"Is the Widowmaker the gun or the man?"

The two men standing looked over at him, saw the gun in his hand, and tried to bring their guns to bear.

Locke calmly shot the first man in the chest, driving him onto his back across the poker table. He immediately turned his attention to the second man, and fired again. The bullet punched into the man's stomach, widening his eyes, causing his hand to open and his gun to hit the floor a moment before he did.

Suddenly, it was quiet. The third man stood there facing Locke with money clenched in his hands. Locke holstered his gun.

"Your choice," he said. "Put the money down."

"You've still got your gun," Locke said. "Use it."

"Hey," the man said, "w-wait a minute. Gimme a chance—"

"You've got a chance," Locke said. "The same chance your friends had."

"But look—it was just some money—"

"Do it!" Locke commanded.

The man flinched, then went for his gun.

Locke drew and fired . . .

THE
WIDOWMAKER
BOOK ONE
INVITATION TO A HANGING

ROBERT J. RANDISI

POCKET STAR BOOKS

NEW YORK LONDON TORONTO SYDNEY SINGAPORE

This book is a work of fiction. Names, characters, places and incidents are products of the author's imagination or are used fictitiously. Any resemblance to actual events or locales or persons, living or dead, is entirely coincidental.

An *Original* Publication of POCKET BOOKS

 A Pocket Star Book published by
POCKET BOOKS, a division of Simon & Schuster, Inc.
1230 Avenue of the Americas, New York, NY 10020

ISBN: 0-7434-7679-4

First Pocket Books printing December 2003

10   9   8   7   6   5   4   3   2   1

POCKET STAR BOOKS and colophon are registered trademarks of Simon & Schuster, Inc.

Cover design by Min Choi

Manufactured in the United States of America

For information regarding special discounts for bulk purchases, please contact Simon & Schuster Special Sales at 1-800-456-6798 or business@simonandschuster.com.

To the members of the online Campfire group. We help each other keep at least one foot in the Western world every day.

THE
WIDOWMAKER

BOOK ONE

INVITATION TO A HANGING

PROLOGUE

Tombstone, Arizona
October 30, 1880

There was a judge, and what appeared to be a jury. All they needed was an executioner.

But actually it was a meeting of the Tombstone Town Council, and Ted Newberry wasn't really a judge, he was just overseeing the proceedings. All of the council members were in attendance, and it was open to the public. It had all the trappings of a public trial.

And John Locke was the defendant.

Marshal of Tombstone was the first job John Locke had ever taken upholding the law. He'd waited until he was forty-five years old to get behind the badge, and for six months he'd kept the peace. His reputation had been made over the years as a bounty hunter, a scout, a gun for hire. He'd held as many different jobs as a fighting man could hold, but never a lawdog until the people of Tombstone asked him to be their marshal. And he'd done a good job, to his way of thinking. He'd upheld the law and was in the process of cleaning up the town when suddenly the people who had hired him—the Tombstone Town Council—became upset about the way he was doing the job.

For the first time in years Tombstone was livable. However, there were factions in town who didn't like Locke's methods, and they seized on the first opportunity to try to get rid of him. Apparently, they were satisfied with only six months worth of quiet.

That evening Locke had been making his rounds, as usual. He often left the office at the first sign of dusk, so that darkness would be falling as he finished up his rounds and reached the Bird Cage. By then the Cage was brightly lit and brimming with music.

He entered and approached the bar. The crystal chandeliers had the place brightly lit. In the corner two girls were taking men downstairs to their rooms, getting an early start. Above him, in the "bird cage" boxes, other women were entertaining men in a more public forum. The stage was lit, but there were no performers yet. Later, there would be dancing girls.

"Marshal," the bartender said.

"Beer."

"Comin' up."

Locke turned and looked the room over. Everything seemed quiet and if the three men had not walked in at that moment he would have had his beer and left. A difference of a few minutes, but then it probably would have happened the next day, or the day after that.

The three men had obviously been to the Bird Cage before and knew their way around, but Locke didn't recognize them. They wore trail clothes, and although they wore guns in holsters, were most likely cowboys, not gunhands. But lots of cowboys knew how to use guns. Locke had lived this long by never underestimating anyone.

"Here ya go, Marshal," the bartender said, setting a frothy mug in front of him.

"Thanks, Slick."

He turned, mug in hand, and continued to survey the room. The three cowboys had approached a poker table, where there was one empty seat. One of the men sat, and the other two took positions standing close to the table. The game was in full swing, there was a lot of money on the table. Off in another corner Doc Holliday's faro table was still covered. Doc was probably in his hotel room with Kate. Of all the men in Tombstone he'd met, Doc came the closest to being what he considered a friend.

Locke finished his beer, but did not like the way the three men were working the poker game. It was a game where money was played, not chips. He suspected they were going to make a grab for the money and try to make a quick getaway. He reached down for his gun, lifted it and let it fall back into the holster. When the first man made a grab for the cash he was ready.

It was the seated man. Right in the middle of a big pot he leaned forward and reached for the bills. They wouldn't have gotten a fortune by any means, but apparently enough to satisfy the trio.

While their partner grabbed the money the other two men cleared leather. Even though they looked like cowboys they moved as if they'd rehearsed this, or done it countless times before. But they hadn't counted on marshal John Locke anticipating their actions.

He drew his gun as the other card players pushed their chairs back and raised their hands.

"Don't!" he shouted.

The two standing men looked over at him, saw his gun in his hand, and tried to bring their guns to bear. Most of the other men and women in the place hit the floor, dreading the gun play.

Locke calmly shot the first man in the chest, driving him onto his back across the poker table. He immediately turned his attention to the second man and fired again before that one could trigger his weapon. The bullet punched into the man's stomach, widening his eyes, causing his hand to open and his gun to hit the floor a moment before he did.

Suddenly, it was quiet. The third man stood there facing Locke with money clenched in his hands. Locke holstered his gun.

"Your choice," he said. "Put the money down."

The man opened his fists and the money fluttered and clattered to the floor.

"You've still got your gun," Locke said. "Use it." He had no doubt that in order to get out of the Bird Cage with the money the three men would have shot anyone who got in their way, including him. He deserved whatever he got.

"Hey," the man said, "w-wait a minute. Gimme a chance—"

"You've got a chance," Locke said. "The same chance your friends had."

"But look—it was just some money—"

"Do it!" Locke commanded.

The man flinched, then went for his gun. If he'd been faster the flinch would still have cost him his life, anyway. As it was he had no chance at all.

Locke drew and fired. . . .

"If we can all find our seats we can call this meeting to order," Ted Newberry shouted.

Locke was seated already, watching the others mill about and avoid his eyes. He knew this was just a formality. They were going to take his badge away from him for sure and there was nothing he could do about it. After all, they had appointed him to the job of marshal, and they could take it away just as easily. Except that they had literally begged him to take the job and now, six months later, he was damned if he'd beg to keep it.

Ted Newberry—who owned the largest store in town—banged his gavel and called out, "Can we get some quiet in here? Take your seats, please."

Sure, Locke thought, not a trial but there's a judge wielding his gavel and calling for order.

The members of the council went up and took their places on either side of Newberry, the Town Council president. They exchanged glances with him, and with each other, but continued to avoid looking at John Locke.

Newberry brought his gavel down again. "This is supposed to be a public meeting, but if you don't quiet down I'll have the lot of you removed."

Yeah, Locke thought, by who? He was the marshal, the

man in charge of keeping the peace—at least, until they took the badge away. If he didn't clear the room, who would?

Finally, the room fell silent and, as all eyes settled on him at once, he thought he could feel their weight pinning him to the chair.

"We're here to decide whether or not John Locke should continue to hold the position as marshal of Tombstone. In light of the fact that he's killed some ten men since he took office, one of them by—"

"All but one in the line of duty," one member of the council felt bound to point out.

"That may be true," Newberry said, "but there might have been other ways to get the job done."

Locke stood up and said, "This is a farce."

"What?" Newberry asked. "Marshal Locke, you did not ask to be recog——"

"And I didn't ask for this job, either," Locke said, cutting the older man off. "You people begged me to take it."

"We did not consider that your idea of upholding the law meant killing," Newberry pointed out. "We wanted a marshal, not a widowmaker—"

"When you offered me the job you knew my reputation," Locke pointed out. The Widowmaker name had become associated with him years before after a newspaper article had used the name, although no one knew if it actually referred to the man, or his gun. "You knew I wore a gun, and you knew I'd use it to do my job whenever I thought it was necessary."

"If you had to, yes," Newberry said. "But Mr. Locke, it's

my observation that you enjoy using your gun. That's not a trait I would look for in a lawman."

"It's what you were looking for six months ago," Locke pointed out.

"Times have changed."

"In six months? This is still Tombstone, Ted. Without me this town will explode inside another six months."

"I rather doubt that," Newberry said. "Nevertheless, it won't be your concern, unless this council votes for you to keep the job." Newberry looked up and down the table at his colleagues. "In light of the incidents that took place in the Bird Cage several nights ago I think it's time to call for a vote. All those in favor—"

"I'll save you the trouble, Ted," Locke said, stepping forward. He removed the marshal's badge from his shirt and dropped it on the table in front of the man. "You can have the badge back."

"You're resigning, then?"

"One step ahead of the chopping block, I'd say," Locke replied. "I know when I'm not wanted. All these years I resisted wearing a badge, because I'd seen too many lawmen standing up for a town that wouldn't back them. You folks assured me that wouldn't happen here, but six months later you not only won't back me, you want me out. You've proven to me I was right all those years. Being a town lawman, be it sheriff or marshal, is a thankless job, and one I'll never take on again."

John Locke put his hat on, turned and headed for the door, but he only got halfway across the room before he turned back.

"Just remember, I won't come back to this job, not if you come crawling on your hands and knees. And I'll say it again and you mark my words . . . without me, or somebody like me, to hold the lid on, this town will explode within six months."

With that Locke finished his walk across the room to the door and barged through it.

The room remained silent. The members of the council stared at the marshal's badge on the table.

Ted Newberry cleared his throat and said, "Very well, then, uh, on to the next order of business, voting on who will be appointed the new marshal of Tombstone. I have nominated Virgil Earp for the job. All those in favor . . ."

When Locke got outside he found Doc Holliday waiting for him.

"Ah notice you're not wearin' your badge anymore," Doc said, in his southern drawl.

"I threw it at them, Doc," Locke said. "It was a mistake for me to take it in the first place. I'm no lawdog."

"Ah coulda tol' you that before."

"I know." Locke put out his hand and Doc took it. "You take care. I'm heading right out. Don't want to stay another minute."

"What am ah supposed to do for a friend?" Doc asked. "You're about the only man in this town I never wanted to kill."

"Try the Earps. I'm sure they'll give my badge to one of them. Probably Virgil."

Doc made a face. "Wyatt's about the only one of them ah can stomach."

"Wyatt, then," Locke said. "He's a strong man. He'll make you a good friend, and you him."

Locke started to walk away but Doc said, "John."

Locke turned.

"What happened the other night," Doc said, "it could have happened to anyone."

"It didn't happen to anyone, Doc," Locke said. "It happened to me."

"And what are you going to do now?"

"I don't know," Locke said. "Maybe I'll head for ol' Mexico, just stay down there for a while."

"How you fixed for funds?"

"Won't need much down there," Locke said.

"When will you come back?"

Locke shrugged. "Months, maybe years."

Doc coughed into a handkerchief, then folded it and tucked it deep inside his vest pocket.

"Ah'll be dead by then," he said, "one way or another."

Locke didn't argue the point. Doc *would* die, one way or another. All men did, but the southern dentist with a quick temper and a quicker gun probably wouldn't out-live many.

They shook hands again and Locke walked to the livery, where he'd already saddled his horse and stowed his gear. He was bound and determined to leave Tombstone behind him as soon as possible.

Tombstone exploded, all right, but John Locke had been wrong. It hadn't taken six months, but almost a year to the day when, on October 26, 1881, the shootout occurred that for years would be known as the Gunfight at the O.K. Corral. As a result much of the Clanton gang ended up dead. Later, Morgan Earp was killed. The Earps left Tombstone then, along with Doc Holliday, but only to hunt down Johnny Ringo and what was left of the Clantons, to take their revenge.

Lives were destroyed, or lost, and it all might have been avoided if John Locke still had been marshal of Tombstone.

ONE

Fredericksburg, Texas
1886

John Locke did not ride into Fredericksburg, Texas, undetected.

"That's him," Gordon Vestal said to his partner, Ed Hansen. "That's the Widowmaker."

The two men were standing in front of the general store they owned together.

"I thought the Widowmaker was the gun?" Hansen asked.

Vestal waved a hand and said, "The man, the gun, what's the difference. The point is he's the man we need to keep the lid on this town."

"I hope you're right."

John Locke rode by them, a very tall man who sat his horse with a ramrod back. He was wearing a black, flat-brimmed Stetson without adornment, a blue shirt with a red bandana tied around his neck, black leather vest, and black trousers. He must have been wearing a gun but they couldn't see it as his left side was to them, and he was probably right-handed. His profile looked as if it had been chiseled from stone. The only indications that he was human were the sweat stains that the August heat had caused beneath his arms.

Vestal looked at Hansen and said, "Of course I'm right. Remember, this is the man who predicted the O.K. Corral. If Tombstone had been able to hold onto him as marshal that never would have happened."

"I heard they fired him."

"He walked away," Vestal said, "when they wouldn't back him."

"Not what I heard."

"What's it matter, Ed?" Vestal asked. "We sent for him and he's here. That's what's important."

They watched as Locke rode past them without a glance and continued on to the end of town where the livery stable was located.

"He looks old," Hansen said.

"Fifty," Vestal said, "maybe. After the life he's lead, that's a testament to the kind of man he is."

"What's he been doing since he left Tombstone?"

"Laying low, I heard," Vestal said. "Some said he got real disillusioned by that whole experience. It was the only time he ever wore a badge."

"Maybe he ain't got it in him anymore," Hansen said. "What do we do then, d'you suppose, if I'm right?"

"I don't know," Vestal said. "Cross that bridge when we come to it, I guess. But right now let's get the others. This is it. We got to make a good enough offer so he takes the job."

"That's your part in all this," Ed Hansen said. "You're the man with the golden tongue, Gordy."

"Well," Vestal said, "I guess we're about to find out just how golden my tongue is."

TWO

After fifty years on this earth John Locke had been enthusiastic, disillusioned, elated, exhausted, rich, poor, sick, well, happy, sad . . . but for the most part none of those emotions ever stayed with him for very long. Immediately following the Tombstone experience his anger had faded and, following the whole O.K. Corral debacle, it had disappeared entirely. However, it had been replaced by . . . well, nothing.

Nothing was what John Locke was feeling as he rode down the main street of Fredericksburg. He'd been contacted about possibly doing a job and promised a fee simply for a consultation. If he decided not to take the job he was free to keep the money and leave.

Locke had taken no jobs from the time he gave up his badge until he read about the O.K. Corral shootout. He had gone to Mexico, found himself a little town where he could live for little or no money, and just ate, drank, and existed. The people there had been happy to have *El Viudador*—the Widowmaker—among them. To have such a man in their village meant that others of his kind would stay away. They were saddened when he decided to leave.

Upon his return, Locke took up residence in New Mexico. He had come to like the food he subsisted on in Mexico very much—as well as the women—and he was able to continue to have access to both while living in Las Vegas. However, his appearance in Las Vegas did not go unnoticed, and he began to receive offers of work. He turned down those which offered him a badge, and took only those that were interesting. He did not hire out as a gunman, bounty hunter, lawman, or mercenary, and he let that be known.

He was still living in Las Vegas, New Mexico, when he received the summons from Fredericksburg, a letter from a man named Gordon Vestal, who claimed that he spoke for the entire Town Council. Locke, with no reason to doubt the man, agreed to ride to Fredericksburg and listen to their offer.

Locke got himself a room at the Main Street Hotel near City Hall, but did not immediately go there to announce his arrival. Instead, he went in search of a mug of beer and a palatable meal. Good meals, he had found over the years, were hard to come by. If he went looking for one in every town he visited he would invariably be disappointed. So, instead, he went in search of meals which were edible—and often was pleasantly surprised with a good one.

There was a café next to the hotel and across from City Hall and he figured, why not? He found a table where he could not only sit with his back to a wall, but see out the window, as well. When the waiter came over he ordered enchiladas, rice, and refried beans.

"And cerveza," he added. "Muy frio."

"Sí, señor."

As the waiter walked away Locke saw two men approaching the café. Neither was wearing a holster, but he could see from the cut of one man's jacket that he was wearing a gun in a shoulder rig. He reached down, eased his customized Colt from his holster to make sure it wouldn't stick if he needed it. He caressed the specially made grip of the pistol, the grooves his fingers would fill if he were to produce the gun. Although he knew it was loaded he checked all six cylinders, then holstered the gun. He'd had the grip custom-made to fit his hand perfectly, giving him no chance of having the weapon ever slip from his hand, as it had once in his youth, when his hand was shaky and sweating. After he'd survived that incident, he had the grip adjusted. Convinced his weapon was ready he waited for the two men to reach the door.

"Let me do the talking," Gordon Vestal said as he and his partner reached the door of the café.

"That won't be a problem," Hansen said.

Vestal looked at him and asked, "Are you scared, Ed?"

"To death."

"I thought you were the one who said he looked old."

"Shh, not so loud!" Ed Hansen hissed. "And all I did was ask what if he was too old."

Vestal smiled and led the way into the café.

THREE

Locke watched the two men enter, sitting relaxed. From their demeanor they were no threat. Besides, one of them looked scared out of his wits.

"Mr. Locke?" one of them asked—the one with the gun under his arm.

"I'm John Locke."

"Gordon Vestal, sir," Vestal said. He extended his hand, but Locke did not take it. "And this is my partner, Ed Hansen. I'm the man who wrote to you—"

"I'm about to have something to eat, Mr. Vestal."

"I see," Vestal said. "Well, that's all right, we don't mind discussing business while we—" He was pulling a chair out to sit when Locke stopped him.

"I don't discuss business while I eat, Mr. Vestal."

Vestal stopped, his hand still on the chair.

"Well, uh, naturally you understand that we are, uh, anxious to get this matter taken care of—"

"No, I don't know that, Mr. Vestal," Locke said, cutting the man off again. "I don't know what the problem is, and I don't want to until after I've eaten."

"Uh, yes, of course."

"Gordon," Hansen said, plucking at his partner's sleeve, "maybe we should let the man eat."

"Yes, all right," Vestal said, grudgingly. "Mr. Locke, I can call a meeting of the Town Council at a moment's notice, if you'll just tell me when—"

"Where will you be?" Locke asked.

"At our store, down the street—"

"Fine," Locke said. "I'll come by when I'm ready."

Vestal seemed frustrated at not being able to complete a sentence, but his partner was still tugging at his sleeve like a small boy, anxious to run away.

"We'll be there, waiting, Mr. Locke," Hansen assured him.

As the two men turned to leave Locke suddenly said, "The money."

"I beg your pardon?" Vestal asked.

"The consultation fee?"

"Oh, the, uh, five hundred dollars I promised you."

"Yes," Locke said, "do you have it with you?"

"Well," Vestal said, touching the breast of his jacket. Apparently he had the money in the pocket on the same side as his gun. "Actually, I do—"

"I'll take it now."

"Well . . . I thought we'd pay you when we met—"

"I get the five hundred whether I take the job or not, right?"

"That's correct."

"Then you can give it to me now." Locke held out his hand.

Vestal continued to hesitate as Hansen nudged him and said, "Give it to him!"

"All right!" Vestal hissed, finally displaying some impatience. Locke thought the two men acted like a married couple more than partners.

"And when you put your hand inside your jacket, Mr. Vestal," Locke said, "bring it out slowly."

"I beg your par——"

"I want to see an envelope, or some cash," Locke went on, "but not a gun. Comprende?"

"You have a gun?" Hansen asked, incredulously.

"The money, please," Locke said.

"Yes, of course." Vestal put his hand inside his jacket and slowly removed a brown envelope. He laid it in Locke's left palm. At that moment the waiter appeared with a plate of steaming food.

"That'll be all, gentlemen," Locke said. "I'll see you after my meal."

"Yes," Vestal said, "all right."

As they turned to leave Hansen said in a low but strenuous tone, "Why did you bring a gun?"

"Not here!" Vestal snapped, as they went out the door.

Locke folded the envelope without counting the contents, put it in his shirt pocket, and bent to the task of eating.

FOUR

After what turned out to be one of the good meals Locke took a turn around Fredericksburg. He didn't know the history of the town, or if it even had one, but that didn't matter. He'd been through enough history, known enough men who made history, good or bad. Men who were larger than life, more myth than man. Men like the Earps. He'd known Virgil and Morgan and Wyatt in Tombstone, and he knew that after he took off his badge and left that town the Earps were going to take it over. He also knew that there were factions in Tombstone which would resist the Earps, and that the result would be bloodshed.

He was still convinced if he had stayed on as marshal it wouldn't have happened at all, but that was in the past. Now he was in Fredericksburg. He'd just had a satisfactory meal and there was the possibility of a job waiting for him, and that was all that concerned him, at the moment.

He touched the envelope in his shirt pocket. He had not yet taken the money out and counted it. It was easy money, though, payment in advance just for listening.

He walked farther down the street until he came to the general store, and stepped inside. There were clerks behind the counter, including the frightened partner, Ed Hansen.

"Oh, Mr. Locke," Hansen said, blinking rapidly. He looked away from the gray-haired woman he was waiting on.

"That's okay," Locke said. "Finish up with your customer, first."

"Uh, oh, yes," Hansen said, "of course."

"That's quite all right," the woman said. "I'm still trying to decide between two fabrics." She looked up at Locke. "I'm making a dress for my daughter, you see."

"How nice for her," Locke said. "She's a lucky girl."

"Why, thank you. Sometimes I don't believe she thinks so."

"She'll learn," Locke said, kindly, "in time." He turned his attention to Hansen.

"Uh, are you ready to, uh, meet with the council?" the man asked him.

"I am," Locke said. "I had a look around town, walked off my meal . . . I'm ready to do business."

"Good, good," Hansen said. "I'll talk to my partner. We can meet within the hour at the City Hall. The other members of the council are anxious to meet you."

"I'll be at the Main Street Hotel," Locke said.

"We'll come for you there, then, when we're ready."

"Fine," Locke said. He tipped his hat to the lady, nodded, and left the store.

"Who is that nice man?" the woman asked, following Locke's progress out the door.

"Oh, believe me, Mrs. Bellington," Hansen said, "you don't want to know."

FIVE

Vestal and Hansen found John Locke sitting in a straight-backed wooden chair on the front porch of his hotel. He had one ankle resting on the other knee and was working on a quirly.

"Gentlemen," he said.

"We're ready to take you over," Vestal said.

Locke dropped his foot to the boardwalk and used that boot to grind out his cigarette.

"Am I meeting with all of the Town Council?" he asked.

"Well, of course," Hansen said, emboldened by the fact that he'd already had one civil exchange with Locke. "They all have to meet you and approve—"

Vestal gave his partner a nudge to shut him up, but it was already too late.

"Approve?" Locke asked, frowning. "I don't think you understand. I've dealt with town councils before. I'm not here to be approved by them. I'm here to see if I will accept the job they—and you—are offering."

"Of course, of course," Vestal said, trying to placate Locke. "My partner doesn't understand, Mr. Locke. Of course there's no approval necessary. The job is yours if you want it. The council understands that. They want only to present the job for your consideration."

Locke gave Hansen a look that made a cold spot form in his belly and grow.

"Can we, uh, go now?" Vestal asked.

Locke looked at him and said, "Sure, lead the way."

Locke followed the two men across the street, into the building and into a first floor room that held seven other men, all seated at a long desk. The layout was similar to the last time he'd faced such an assemblage in Tombstone, but the situation was different. Here he was the one in total control.

"Gentlemen," Gordon Vestal announced, "this is John Locke."

"This is the man you said can help us with our problem?" one of the men asked.

It did not surprise Locke to see that the speaker was the youngest man in the room.

"Who are you?" Locke asked.

Taken aback for a moment the man finally said, "Uh, I'm Harry Selkirk."

"What business do you own?" Locke asked.

"Uh, I own the hardware store."

"Have you owned it long?"

"Only a few months. Why?"

"I'm just wondering how much longer you'd own it if I turned around and walked out of this room."

"Now wait a minute—"

"Shut up, Selkirk," another man said. Of the seven men seated he was the middle one. He also appeared to be the oldest.

"Mr. Locke, I'm Judge Ansel Tinsley, president of this council. We're grateful that you've agreed to come and see us today."

"Mr. Vestal indicated you folks had a problem you couldn't solve," Locke said. "Why don't you just tell me what it is?"

"Mr. Hansen?" the Judge said. "You're not a member of this council. Would you leave, please?"

"Now wait a minute—" Hansen started, but his partner cut him off.

"Never mind, Ed," Vestal said. "You know only members of the Town Council can attend meetings. Everyone else needs an invitation."

"So invite me."

Locke turned and looked at Hansen. The look was enough to drive the younger partner from the room.

Vestal walked up to the table and took his place in a chair at the end.

"Mr. Locke," Judge Tinsley asked, "do you know who Ignacio Colon is?"

"Colon is probably the most bloodthirsty bandido in all of New Mexico and Mexico," Locke said, "but especially Texas."

"Exactly."

"Seems to me he's been terrorizing these parts for years," Locke went on. "Specifically southern Texas."

"Indeed," Judge Tinsley said.

"I also remember hearing that Francisco Razo was riding with him," Locke said, "and Carlos Mendoza, as well."

"To name but two," Judge Tinsley said. "You're well informed. I appreciate that."

"And what has all of this got to do with your particular problem?" Locke asked. "You've got your own sheriff, don't you?"

"Indeed we do."

"So you don't need me to track these desperados down."

"No."

"Then . . . ?"

Tinsley leaned forward and clasped his hands together, staring intently at Locke.

"Mr. Locke, what would you say if I told you we already had Ignacio Colon in our jail, and that we intend to hang him?"

Without hesitation Locke replied, "I'd say that if you have him in your jail you should have hanged him by now, before his boys come for him and burn your nice little town to the ground."

SIX

"We can't just string him up from a tree," the judge said. "This has to be done right."

"Has he had a trial?"

"Yes, he has," Judge Tinsley said, "a fair trial. I presided over it myself. He was found guilty and sentenced to die."

"So what's the problem?" Locke asked. "Hang him. I assume you're going to do it here?"

"Yes," Tinsley said, "that was part of his sentence. He's to hang here so our citizens can witness it. But we need time."

"Time for what?"

"Time to build the gallows," Tinsley said, "and time for the right people to be invited."

"Invited?"

"Yes," the judge said, "and that's the job we want to hire you for."

"You want me to invite people to a hanging?"

"In part," Judge Tinsley said. "You see, we need someone who will oversee the entire process and make sure that everything goes off without a hitch."

"What do you mean, everything?"

"There are people who need to be present," the judge said. "We'll need invitations sent."

Locke frowned. He'd heard of sending invitations out to hangings, but had never been involved with such a thing before.

"Who are these people?" he asked.

"Family members of the people Colon and his men killed, people who have suffered great losses and need to know that this man will not plague them ever again."

"What else would you need?"

"You'd be a master of ceremonies, of sorts, as well as making sure the invitations go out, the gallows is built correctly, Colon doesn't escape—"

"Whoa, hold it," Locke said. "Don't you have a sheriff?"

"Yes, of course," the judge said. "The sheriff who arrested Colon."

"Then isn't it his responsibility to make sure the prisoner doesn't escape?"

"Yes, normally it would be," Judge Tinsley said, "but if you take this job we'd like you to be involved in every aspect of this execution, and that means making sure Colon makes it to the hanging, alive and well."

"I see."

"Now, we all know your reputation, Mr. Locke, so there's no question that you are the man we want," Tinsley said. "The question then becomes, do you want the job?"

Locke turned it all over in his mind for a few moments. Adding into his prospective duties some of the sheriff's job sounded suspicious to him, but the work itself was not without appeal. It was different from anything he'd done before, and that was exactly what he looked for, these days.

"Judge," he said, "I'd like to do one more thing before I make my decision."

"And what's that?"

"I'd like to talk to Colon."

The men at the table began to murmur and the judge silenced them with a quick chopping motion of his hand.

"The man has a right to make his own stipulations," he announced. "We'll give him everything he needs to make his decision." The man looked at Locke. "If you'll wait outside, sir, we'll have someone take you over to the prisoner."

"Thank you."

"Mr. Locke."

"Yes?"

"Will you be making your decision immediately afterward," the judge asked, "or will you need more time?"

"No," Locke said. "I think I'll be able to give you my decision right after I speak to Colon."

"In that case," the judge said, "we shall stay in session and wait for you here."

SEVEN

Locke was waiting patiently outside when a man with a badge approached him. He looked midthirties, average height and slender. His appearance was more in keeping with that of a storekeeper than a lawman.

"Mr. Locke? Sheriff Ray Horrigan."

"Sheriff."

The two men sized each other up and did not share a handshake.

"If you'll follow me I'll take you to see the prisoner."

Horrigan led Locke down the street to his office, where he grabbed the keys from a peg on the wall and proceeded back to the cell block.

"He's the only prisoner we've got, right now."

"Are you expecting his men to try to break him out?" Locke asked.

"Oh, yes," Horrigan said.

"Then why not move him?"

Horrigan turned and looked at Locke.

"Well, that'll be your decision, won't it?" he asked. "I mean, if you accept this . . . position?"

"I won't be taking your job."

"No," Horrigan said, "you won't." He pushed open the door to the cell block. "He's all yours. I guess you can pretty much introduce yourselves."

"Thanks."

Locke stepped through the door and Horrigan closed and locked it behind him. Through a small barred slot in the door he said, "Just knock when you want to get out."

Locke nodded and turned toward the cells. There were three in a row, and only the center one was occupied. The man in it was lying on the cot, hands behind his head, as if he was lounging in the sun.

"Buenos días, señor," he said.

"Buenos días," Locke said, returning the greeting. "¿Señor Ignacio Colon?"

"Sí," the imprisoned man said, "I am Ignacio Ricardo De La Vega Colon, at your service." Somehow the man managed to execute a bow while lying down. It was obvious from the way his feet hung off the end of the cot that he was a tall man. He was in his thirties, very tall, with big hands and feet. When he spoke gold winked from his mouth. He had many days' growth of stubble that was on its way to becoming a beard.

"And you, señor?" Colon asked. "¿Cómo se llama?"

"My name is John Locke."

"Aye, Dios." Colon sat up, drew his legs up, and rested his forearms on his knees. "I have heard this name before. You are a very famous man, no?"

"Depends on your definition of fame."

"Sí, John Locke," Colon went on. "You are he who they call El Viudador. Sí, señor, you are muy famoso."

Locke just shrugged.

"Señor, to what do I owe the honor of this visit?"

"I've been asked to . . . officiate at your hanging, Señor Colon."

"Ah," Colon said, his eyes lighting up, "you are to be my bastonero, eh?"

"Bastonero?"

"Sí, it is what we call it in my country. You are—cómo se dice—ah, my master of ceremonies."

"I suppose you could call it that."

"And have you accepted this exalted position yet?"

"No," Locke said, "not yet. I wanted to see you first."

"Ah, to ask my approval, no?" Colon slapped his hands together and said, "You have it! I approve. I am delighted!"

"And why is that?"

"It is a compliment for one such as you to have been summoned to be sure that I am hanged properly." Colon rose and approached the bars, grasped them firmly with both hands, and thrust his face against them. His golden smile dazzling. Locke had never seen a man with so many gold teeth.

"Also, when I kill you and escape," Colon said, "my own reputation will be so much enhanced, you see?"

"I see," Locke said. "What makes you think you will escape?"

"It is a certainty, señor," Colon said. "These people, they should have strung me up from the closest tree, but no. Instead they give me time to plan my escape, give my men time to plan."

"So if I shot you now?" Locke asked.

"Ah," Colon said, "that would make you an extremely smart man, señor. And it would be my honor to die by the hand of such a man. But I will not let the people of this town kill me." The Mexican turned his head and spat. "Not only would I then be dead, but my reputation would be, as well, and that I cannot allow. You understand?"

"I understand."

"Bueno."

"So you believe I should take this job?"

Colon returned to his cot, gave John Locke an amiable look, spread his hands and said, "Señor, I insist on it."

Locke knocked on the door to the cell block and was let out by the sheriff.

"So what happened—" the man started, but Locke walked past him and went out the door.

As he came back into the council room the members interrupted their conversation, then hurriedly returned to their seats as Locke approached the table.

"So you've had your talk with Colon," Judge Tinsley said. "Have you decided whether or not you will accept this job, Mr. Locke?"

"Judge," Locke said, "I wouldn't miss this for the world."

EIGHT

They offered to give Locke an office in City Hall to work out of but he refused. He said he'd work from the Main Street Hotel. All he asked was that the town pay for his room. They offered to put him up in a better hotel, but he allowed as how the Main Street was just fine for him. The council appointed Gordon Vestal to be Locke's "contact" with the group.

"Anything you need," Judge Tinsley said, "just tell Gordon and he'll get it for you."

Before he left the meeting room he said, "The first thing I need is a list of family members who should be invited."

"We can get that for you," Tinsley said. "I'll have it delivered to your hotel later today."

"And I need to be able to go into any store in town without having to worry about money."

"We will open accounts for you everywhere," the judge said. "Anything else?"

"I'm sure there is," Locke said, "but I'll think of it later."

"Excellent," Tinsley said. He stood and offered Locke his hand. "Then we're finished here?"

"Not exactly," Locke said, ignoring the man's hand. The judge frowned but before he could speak again Locke said, "There's the question of my fee."

Outside Vestal said, "You're quite a negotiator."

"I don't need this job, Mr. Vestal," Locke said, "but apparently, your town does need me."

"Come," Vestal said, "I'll walk you back to your hotel and make the arrangements for your bill."

The two began walking together.

"You mind if I ask you something?"

"No," Locke said, "as long as it's not about Tombstone." He looked at the storekeeper. "I don't talk about that."

"That's fine," Vestal said. "It's actually not about that."

"All right, then."

"I'm curious about this job," Vestal said. "What made you take it? It wasn't the money."

"What makes you think not?"

"You had already decided to take it before you discussed money. You knew it when you came back. What was it?"

"Colon."

"Did he tweak your ego?"

"Ego has nothing to do with it," Locke said. "I found him . . . intelligent, charming, arrogant . . . and very interesting. In fact, the whole situation interests me. But mostly, I took this job because I've never had one like it before."

"Ah, I see," Vestal said. "I guess it's important for a man like you—or any man—to stir his life up now and then."

"Exactly," Locke said. "If your life isn't interesting, what good is it?"

"I understand perfectly."

Locke doubted that a storekeeper would understand a man like him, at all, but he kept that to himself.

"Where's your partner?"

"Probably back at the store. One of us usually has to be there at all times."

When they reached the hotel they entered together and Vestal went right to the desk. He spoke with the clerk, then turned to Locke as the man behind the desk left his post.

Vestal came back to Locke and said, "He's getting the manager. I'll introduce you and then I have to get back to my store before my partner runs it into the ground."

"Doesn't sound like a very good partner."

"He's okay," Vestal said. "He's very good at paperwork, which I hate."

"Guess everybody's got to be good at something."

The clerk reappeared with an older man behind him. Balding but mightily mustachioed, the man approached Vestal and Locke.

"Sam Ferguson, this is John Locke."

"Mr. Locke," Ferguson said, shaking Locke's hand, "welcome to the Main Street."

"Mr. Locke now works for the Town Council, Sam," Vestal said. "That means he gets whatever he wants, free of charge."

"Free?" Ferguson asked, raising eyebrows which, if combed back, might have solved his baldness problem.

"Don't worry," Locke said. "I won't abuse the privilege."

"Well, uh, what do you want? A bigger room?"

"No," Locke said, "the room I have is fine. I just don't want to be presented with a bill when I eat, or when I check out."

Ferguson looked at Vestal.

"The council will pay all of Mr. Locke's expenses."

"All right, then," Ferguson said, with a shrug. "I don't care who pays as long as I get my money."

"Good," Vestal said, "then that's settled. Thanks, Sam."

"Sure," Ferguson said, and retreated into the bowels of his hotel.

"Well," Vestal said, "anything else that comes to mind let me know."

"I will."

"And if you need to be outfitted for any reason just come over to the store and take your pick."

"You know," Locke said, "if you'd hired the wrong man and opened your town up to him like this it could have been a disaster."

"Well then," Vestal said, "we hired the right man, didn't we?"

"I guess that will be up to you to decide when this is all over, won't it?"

"As long as Colon's neck stretches," Vestal said, "we'll be satisfied, don't worry."

When Vestal was halfway out the door Locke said, "Don't forget to get me that list."

"It's on its way."

"Oh, and where is there a printer in town?"

"A printer?"

"Yeah," Locke said, "if I'm going to send out invitations I'll need a printer."

Vestal stepped back into the lobby and thought for a moment.

"The only place I can think of to get something printed would be the newspaper office," Vestal said. "The *Fredericksburg Front Page,* it's called. Just go over and tell the editor there to consult me on anything you want. I'll be sure you get it."

"All right," Locke said. "Where's the office?"

Vestal gave Locke simple directions to follow, after which he went out the door and started back to his store.

Locke decided to go into the saloon attached to the hotel and see if word had spread yet that he was to have anything he wanted.

"Help ya?" the bartender asked. The place was about half filled, but as Locke entered from the hotel lobby other men were entering through a door from the street. It was getting to be that time of the day.

"A beer," Locke said. "A cold one."

"Only kind we serve."

The barman drew a beer and returned with it. He looked enough like the owner to be his brother.

"On the house, Mr. Locke," the man added with a smile. "Word travels fast."

"Especially when you're one of the owners," the bartender said. "You spoke with my brother Sam." He stuck out his hand. "I'm Pat, the one with the hair."

Locke shook his hand.

"Guess you're in town to help us out with our problem."

"Problem?"

"Hanging Ignacio Colon."

"Does everybody know about that?"

"Everybody knows we got to hang him," Pat said. "And everybody knows it ain't gonna be easy. Pretty soon everybody'll know that you're here to make sure it gets done."

Locke said, "I guess so."

Pat went to serve some other customers and Locke worked on his beer, wondering if having "everybody" know his business was such a good thing?

NINE

He spent the entire evening in his room after having that one beer. The hotel had once seen better times, a fact that was well illustrated by the faded look of the walls and furnishings. The bed was solid, though, which was really all he cared about. He relaxed, both before and after the list of invitees was delivered to him by a deputy.

"Are you really the Widowmaker?" the young lawman asked.

Locke closed the door in his face. The list of names was longer than he had thought it would be. Ignacio Colon had killed a lot of people—people with large families. Locke read the list over once before removing his boots and taking the time to clean his rifle and pistol thoroughly. He took care of his own weapons, never allowing anyone else to touch them. If one of his guns ever failed him, he would have only himself to blame. After that he made notes for himself concerning the invitations, then turned in and slept soundly through the night until the light of dawn woke him. Well rested and ready for his new job, he took the list with him to breakfast. He found the food sufficiently bad to eliminate the hotel as a future source of nourishment.

It was 9:15 A.M. when he stopped in front of the office of the *Fredericksburg Front Page*. He looked inside the window and saw someone moving about. He opened the door and entered, greeted by the clatter of the press and the smell of ink. A man wearing a long apron was standing in front of the machinery and already had smudges of black on his face and hands. Locke waved, trying in vain to get his attention. He considered firing a shot, but decided that, too, might go unnoticed.

He looked around and saw a door in the back that apparently led to a glass-enclosed office. After one more look at the man running the press Locke walked to that door and knocked on it loud enough to rattle the glass. When no one answered he opened that door and stepped into the room. He closed the door, at least partially muffling the sound of the running press.

The room held a rolltop desk, a long table on which the pages of a not yet assembled newspaper edition were spread, some file cabinets, and chairs, one of which was a vacated desk chair. He wondered if the man at the press doubled as the editor, but at that moment a tall, full-bosomed woman came into the room from a back door and stopped short when she saw him. Her violet eyes widened and she caught her breath, one hand going to her throat. She had a long, pale, slender neck and brown hair pinned into a careless bun with tendrils of hair trailing from it. It was early and she already looked harried.

"Don't be afraid," he said.

"I'm not," she insisted. "You just startled me, that's all."

"I couldn't get the attention of the man outside."

"That's Augustus," she said. "He's deaf, which makes him almost perfect for the job . . . except for one thing."

"What's that?"

"He can't hear it if it jams," she said. "That means he rarely looks away from it."

"Which explains why I couldn't get his attention by waving," Locke said. "Then I knocked on your door here, but no one answered."

"I was in the storeroom and couldn't hear it." She came the rest of the way into the room now that she was no longer startled and approached her desk.

"I'm Nina Ballinger, the owner and editor of the paper. Can I help you?"

"Well, Mrs. Ballinger—"

"It's Miss."

She appeared to be in her thirties, so he'd assumed she was either married or widowed. Either way he'd felt safe with "Mrs."

"I'm sorry," he said, "Miss Ballinger, my name is John Locke. I'm—"

"I know who you are, Mr. Locke." Her attitude changed abruptly. "In fact, I was going to come over to the hotel to see you later today."

"Is that so?"

"Yes," she said, "you see, I'm also the feature reporter for the paper and I wanted to do an interview for the—"

"I'm sorry, Miss Ballinger," he said, interrupting her, "I don't do interviews."

"Mr. Locke, you are the man who predicted the Shootout at the O.K. Corral," she said. "Now, I know you haven't done any interviews since you left Tombstone, or since the shootout, but I thought—"

"Miss Ballinger," he said, "I haven't done any interviews because I don't like talking about that time in my life."

"But didn't you feel justified after the Earps and the Clantons fought it out, covering Tombstone in blood as you said would happen—"

"That question sounds suspiciously like the beginning of an interview, Miss Ballinger."

She studied him, her brow furrowed in frustration.

"Mr. Locke, just why did you come here this morning?"

"I was looking for a place to have some invitations printed up."

"Invitations?"

"Yes," he said. "I need to send out some proper invitations for the Ignacio Colon hanging."

She stared at him silently, this time in either shock or disbelief.

"You are sending out invitations to a hanging?" she finally asked.

"That's right."

"I've heard of this being done, but it isn't very common," she said, lowering her eyes and staring at the floor thoughtfully. Then she looked back at him. "And you want us to print them here?"

"Yes." He dug into his short pocket and pulled out a slip of paper. "I've made some notes about what I'd like the invitations to say—"

"Wait, wait," she said, hastily holding up one hand. "This is a newspaper office, sir. We don't print fliers or invitations."

"Are you doing so well, Miss Ballinger, that you couldn't use the extra business?"

"Are you saying that you would pay well for this printing job?"

"You would be paid, Miss Ballinger," he said, "but by the town, not by me. How much you get paid is between you and them."

She thought a moment, tapping one fingernail against her front teeth while she did so. She was wearing a spotless white shirt that he knew would not stay that way during the course of the day and a blue skirt that covered the tops of a pair of brown boots. Her right foot tapped the floor in time with her fingernail.

"I tell you what, Mr. Locke," she said. "Neither you nor the town has to pay for these invitations."

"No? And why is that, Miss Ballinger?"

"Because I'll make you a bargain."

"What kind of a bargain?"

She walked toward him and stopped within arm's length. He could smell the soap she'd used to wash with that morning.

"I'll print these invitations up in exchange for an interview."

"No."

She blinked.

"That was a quick answer. You don't want to think it over?"

"No."

"Or ask the Town Council about it?"

"No."

"Why not?"

"Because, Miss Ballinger," he said, coldly, "I was assured that this town would give me whatever I needed to get this job done. In fact, I was guaranteed it."

"But I didn't agree—"

He grabbed her hand, startling her again—or perhaps this time frightening her. He didn't much care which. He slapped his notes into her hand.

"Miss Ballinger," he said, "that is what I want in the invitation, and I need twenty copies as soon as possible."

He turned and started for the door.

"Mr. Locke, wait just a minute—"

"This is something you have to take up with your Town Council, Miss Ballinger," he said, "not me."

"But—"

"Good morning."

TEN

Locke was sitting out in front of the Main Street Hotel a few hours later when Judge Tinsley and Gordon Vestal came walking over.

"A moment of your time, Mr. Locke?" the judge asked.

"You're paying for a lot more of my time than that, Judge."

"Uh, yes, of course." Both men stepped up onto the boardwalk and Vestal fetched two more chairs and brought them over so he and the judge could sit.

"If you don't mind," Locke said before they sat, "both on one side, please. Having someone on either side makes me claustrophobic."

"Oh, uh, sure," Vestal said. He moved his chair so that he and Locke were seated with the judge between them.

"Mr. Locke, we appear to have a problem—a mutual problem."

"Does our mutual problem have violet eyes and a very pretty neck?" Locke asked.

"Hmm, yes," the judge said, "I see you have met our esteemed newspaper publisher, Nina Ballinger."

"Quite a woman," Locke said.

"Indeed."

"She's about to ruin this whole deal for you, though."

"Now wait a second," Tinsley said, "we can't let one person alter our agreement in any way."

"Then don't," Locke said. "Get her to print those invitations for me."

"We could send them to Austin. They have a—" Vestal started.

"No," Locke said. "I want them done here."

"But it would only take a few days—"

"A few days more than I'm willing to spend," Locke pointed out. "Remember, Colon's got a gang out there that's not gonna let him go to the gallows easily."

Tinsley and Vestal exchanged worried glances.

"Don't tell me this woman has got you both buffaloed."

Now they both looked at him.

"She's a very independent woman," Judge Tinsley replied.

"Tough," Vestal said. "A very tough lady."

"Which is probably why she's not on the Town Council, eh?"

Both men had the good grace to look guilty. Obviously, the men in town had conspired to keep Nina Ballinger off the council.

"Well, I've got even more respect for her than I did before," Locke said.

"If you would just consent to an interview," Judge Tinsley said, "then she'd print the invitations."

"This seems like such a small point," Vestal said. When

Locke gave him a hard look he added, "Well, I mean, uh, to me . . ."

Locke could have gotten on his horse and left, but it was a small point, and they were paying him a lot of money . . . speaking of which . . .

"About my fee," he said.

"Ah, yes," the judge said, "we're picking up half the money at the bank later today."

They'd agreed that he would receive half before and half after the job was done.

"All right," Locke said. "Tell Miss Ballinger she can have an interview."

Judge Tinsley sat back in his chair and slapped his thigh triumphantly.

"But only—" Locke said, cutting the judge's celebration short, "—only after she prints up the invitations—"

"That's fair," Vestal said.

"—and," Locke continued, waiting quietly until both men were looking at him, "no questions about Tombstone."

The judge and Vestal exchanged a glance. They knew Tombstone was exactly what Nina Ballinger wanted to talk with Locke about.

"Well," Vestal said, "it is an interview."

"Yes," Tinsley said, "yes." He looked at Locke. "I think I will be able to persuade her to avoid that subject."

"And I want one more thing."

Tinsley hesitated, kept himself from looking at Vestal, and asked with trepidation, "What's that?"

"I want Miss Ballinger to have a seat on the council."

"What?" Vestal asked.

"Oh, Mr. Locke—" the judge started.

"Or I ride out of town today."

"This—this is preposterous!" the judge said, inflating his chest for a moment. "Why would you ask for such a thing?"

"Because," Locke said, leaning so close to the judge that the man drew back and deflated his chest, "I can . . . can't I, gentlemen?"

ELEVEN

Before looking for a decent place to have dinner—he'd had lunch at the same place he'd eaten the day before—Locke stopped by the newspaper office again. It was several hours later, and this time the press was quiet, and deaf Augustus was not there. The door to the office stood wide open and Nina Ballinger was sitting at her desk with her back to it. He walked to the door and knocked.

"Come to gloat?" she asked, looking at him over her shoulder.

"Gloat?" he asked. "What do I have to gloat about?"

"Well, I agreed to do the invitations," she said. "You got your way, didn't you?"

"Seems to me you got something, too. In fact, I'd say everything worked out pretty fairly."

She swiveled her chair around so she could see him without straining.

"Fairly? Isn't that just like a man? You got exactly what you wanted, and I didn't. That's your definition of fair, Mr. Locke?"

"He held up the copy of her newspaper he'd picked

up only an hour before. In bold letters the headline read:

WIDOWMAKER IN FREDRICKSBURG.
EXCLUSIVE INTERVIEW TO COME.

"When did you have time to do this?"

She looked sheepish. "Oh, that. I had Augustus set that as soon as you left this morning."

"You were pretty sure of yourself."

"I've dealt with the men in this town for a long time," she explained.

"But not with me."

"I was certain they would do whatever they could to keep you from leaving."

"So you're happy with the result?"

"The question is," she said, turning and grabbing something from her desk, "will you be?"

He took the sheet from her and found himself looking at a printed version of his invitation.

The town of Fredericksburg invites you to the legal execution by hanging of Ignacio Colon . . .

"I'll just need to fill in the time and place, but that's basically it."

"This is good," he said, handing it back. "I approve."

"So when do I get my interview?"

"When do I get my entire order?" he asked.

"As soon as I get a date."

"I'll have it for you tomorrow."

"Then I'll have Augustus run them off right away," she promised. "You'll have them an hour after you give me the date."

He touched the brim of his hat and said, "Thank you, Miss Ballinger."

He started for the door, then stopped and said, "Oh, maybe you could recommend a place in town to get a decent steak?"

"Five blocks west," she said, "there's a place called The Dexter House. It's the best restaurant in town. In fact, most of the members of the Town Council eat there."

"I'll try it," he said, "thanks."

As he reached the door she said, "I was just about to go there myself. Why don't we . . . eat together?"

"Why not?" he said. "But no interview questions."

"Agreed. Just let me lock up."

TWELVE

When Locke and Nina Ballinger entered The Dexter House they suddenly became the center of attention. At a table in the center of the room Locke saw Judge Tinsley eating with Gordon Vestal and a couple of other members of the council. While others in the room turned their attention back to their meals, the four council members followed Locke and Nina with their eyes while they were shown to a table in a corner.

As Locke held Nina's chair for her—surprising her—he was aware that he had not changed his shirt since arriving in town. He made a mental note to take a bath in the morning and haul out a clean shirt.

"Do you always ask for a corner table?" Nina asked, as they were seated.

"Yes."

"And if one is not available?"

"Then I eat someplace where one is."

"That must be a difficult way to live," she said, and then added hurriedly, "That wasn't an interview question, just an observation."

"Observations are allowed."

"Would you like a beer?" she asked.

"No," he said. "Coffee."

She looked up at the attractive young waitress and said, "Two coffees, Gloria."

"Sure, Nina."

"Steak," Locke said.

"What?" Nina and Gloria asked at the same time.

"I'd like a steak, well done, and whatever comes with it."

Gloria looked at Nina, who said, "I'll have the same, but make it rare."

"Comin' up," Gloria said. "Two coffees, two steaks, one burnt and one rare."

"Well done?" Nina asked. "I thought all men ate their steaks rare."

"I'm not all men."

"That's obvious."

She looked over at the center table, where the four men were taking turns glancing over at them.

"Why'd you do it?" she asked.

"Do what?"

She looked at him. "Why did you make them offer me a seat on the council?"

"I didn't like the way they talked about you."

"You don't even know me."

"That doesn't matter," he said. "I was impressed with you. You strike me as the kind of a person who would be an asset to any town."

"I think so," she said, "but not many people—not many men—agree."

"Well, now you have your chance."

"Maybe."

"Why did you say they 'offered' you a seat?" he asked. "Didn't you accept?"

"Not yet," she replied.

"What are you waiting for?"

"If I accept they'll just find a way to vote me off after you've gone. It was a nice gesture on your part, though."

Gloria arrived with their coffee and they fell quiet while she poured. After she left and Locke picked up his cup, Nina did the same and studied him over the rim.

"When you asked about a restaurant," she said, "you weren't . . . hinting that we eat together, were you?"

"No."

She colored slightly, from embarrassment.

"I'm sorry," he said. "You're very attractive, but I'm not here to meet women."

"I understand." She suddenly looked very uncomfortable sitting there with him. It didn't really concern Locke all that much, but the four councilmen were still looking over at them, almost nervously.

"Please don't feel . . . foolish," he said to Nina.

"I'm afraid that's easier said than done," she said. "I'm, uh, I was . . . wrong about you."

"It won't be the last time," he assured her.

"I believe you."

"I'm sure most men are . . . charmed by you, but I'd prefer to have a conversation on equal ground . . . if you don't mind."

Used to having men fawn over her because of her

looks, but not taking her seriously, this prospect made her feel less embarrassed.

"I'd like that, Mr. Locke," she said. "I'd like that very much."

"Good," he said, "then why don't you start by telling me what you know about what's going on in this town."

"Well," she began, "did anyone happen to tell you how the sheriff captured Ignacio Colon?"

THIRTEEN

"**H**e tripped over him."

They had paused in their conversation when the steaks came, and had taken time to eat a few bites. Locke nodded his approval. The meat was cooked to his liking. After Nina tasted hers and nodded to Gloria, the waitress left and the newspaper editor continued to speak.

"What?" Locke asked.

"I said he tripped over him, literally," she said. "It was dumb luck. Colon and his bandits hit a stagecoach just outside of town. The driver brought it in before he died of his wounds, but all the passengers were dead. The sheriff assembled a posse and went after them. The gang split up, and so did the posse. Something must have happened to spook Colon's horse, causing it to throw him. He was unconscious when the sheriff actually tripped over him and fell."

"How do you know all this?"

"I have my sources."

"Tell me more."

"Well, once they had Colon in a cell they rushed him to trial and sentenced him to hang. They knew his gang would be coming for him eventually, and the sheriff doesn't feel competent enough to hold him—and he's right. That man doesn't have the backbone."

"So they needed someone who did."

"And reached out to you."

"Now I get it. Although I haven't formally accepted the sheriff's badge, I'm doing his job."

"Exactly . . . but you knew that when you accepted the position. I mean, you're certainly not a stupid man."

"No," Locke said, "I'm not."

"And you're probably getting paid a lot more than he is," she pointed out. "But you don't strike me as the kind of man who does things just for the money. So why did you take this job?"

He looked across the table at her, swallowed the bite of meat he'd been chewing, and said, "I can't resist a challenge."

"Is that why you took the job as marshal of Tombstone?" she asked.

He smiled. "Nice try."

"Won't be my last," she said, smiling back.

"What took you so long?"

"Vestal and Hansen came to town five years ago, bought the store they now own, and have expanded it twice since then."

"And the judge?"

"The judge is from here."

"How long has he been president of the council?" Locke asked.

"Forever."

"How long has the sheriff had his job?"

"About a year. He took the place of a man Ignacio Colon killed."

"Was that one of the crimes he was convicted of?" Locke asked. "Killing a lawman?"

"Yes, that and many others. He and his men have been terrorizing this area for years."

Locke finished the pie he'd ordered for dessert and poured himself and Nina another cup of coffee each from the pot Gloria had brought them. Nina was still picking at her pie.

"They'll come for him, won't they?" she asked.

"Yes."

"Why wouldn't they just pick a new leader and forget about him?"

"With all the success they've had with Colon?" Locke asked. "They won't give that up so easily."

"Well then, why haven't they tried to get him out yet?" she asked. "He's been in that jail for weeks."

"It could be they're having a hard time choosing a new leader."

"A falling out among thieves?"

"Possibly," Locke said. "Colon's their clear-cut leader. To come and get him they'll have to work together, but someone will still have to lead them. Carlos Mendoza and Francisco Razo also ride with him. They're the types who would like to move up from segundo to leader, if they got the chance."

"You sound like you know them."

"I know their kind," Locke said. "From what I've heard one of them won't easily follow the other."

"But . . . what if Colon is hanged while they're . . . arguing?"

"They probably have someone in town keeping an eye on things," Locke said. "My bet is they know his hanging date hasn't officially been set yet. There's even a chance one or both of them are stalling, hoping that he will hang and they can take over."

"Well," Nina said, pushing her empty plate away, "it's been set now, hasn't it?"

He smiled once again.

FOURTEEN

It was during their dessert that Tinsley, Vestal, and the other two men finished eating, paid their bill, and left—but not without one last glance back at Locke and Nina.

Now Locke said, "The council seems real nervous about you and me eating together."

"I've told you things they left out," she said. "They know that, and they'll be afraid of what you'll do with that knowledge."

"Let 'em be afraid for a while."

"You're going to stick with this job?"

"Right until the end."

"Why?"

"Because I took it on," he said. "I usually finish what I start."

There was a question about Tombstone right on the tip of her tongue and they both knew it.

When they rose to leave they once again attracted attention as they made their way to the door.

"Folks know who you are," she said, outside.

"Thanks in no small part to you," he pointed out.

"I hope you keep your promises with the same zeal with which you finish your jobs."

"Promises?"

"My interview."

"Of course," he said. "You'll have your interview."

"When?"

"As soon as I get this hanging on the way," he said. "I'll need to get the date to you tomorrow and get those invitations out. You print them out for me and you can have your interview tomorrow evening."

Her eyes brightened and she said, "Wonderful!"

He didn't think so. The last interview he'd given had been years ago, when he first took the job as marshal of Tombstone. It had not gone well. Nina Ballinger, however, appeared to be intelligent enough to do a decent job of it.

"I'm going to assume," she said, "that Tombstone is the only subject I have to avoid."

"Yes."

"As much as I'd like to talk about it," she said. "I'm very curious about—"

"Sorry," he said.

"You predicted the O.K. Corral," she said, impressed.

"Not exactly."

"Well," she added, "not precisely, but your prediction of the town exploding was close enough."

"I missed by six months."

She smiled and asked, "Can I quote you?"

"Why not?" he said. "But remember, that's the only Tombstone quote you'll get from me."

"Hey, it's already more than I had hoped."

FIFTEEN

Locke noticed that Nina Ballinger seemed surprised he didn't offer to walk her home, but he'd gotten what he wanted out of her. Walking her home would have been a waste of time for him. It wasn't that he was disinterested in women. And it wasn't that he didn't find her attractive—he did. But he was working and women were for another time.

So they said goodnight in front of The Dexter House and he went in search of a saloon.

The first place he came to didn't seem to have a name, unless it was the sign over the door that read WHISKEY AND GAMBLING. He entered and found the place about three-quarters full. It was not yet completely dark out, and he knew that like most saloons, night would soon bring in the customers.

There were table games aplenty, all of them open for business. He saw faro, blackjack, and roulette, and off to one side there appeared to be two house games of poker going. His game of choice was poker, although he was not averse to a hand or two of blackjack. Tonight, however, his only desire was for a beer. He went to the bar, where there was plenty of room, and waved to the single bartender.

"What?" the man asked, looking bored.

"Beer."

"Comin' up."

Locke eyed the place, on the lookout for potential trouble. For a man in his position, who might be recognized the moment he walked into a saloon, it paid to be aware of his surroundings. If trouble did occur, but did not involve him, he would ignore it. Early in his life he'd interjected himself into other men's troubles a time or two, and it never turned out well. He soon got himself cured of that before it became a habit. Later, when he accepted the badge in Tombstone, it became his job to guard against trouble. As a result he'd killed a few men who thought they'd been cheated and wanted to settle things with a gun. He never liked killing a man unless it was personal—and that included bounty hunting. When he was hunting men it was very personal, because that was how he was making his living. He usually left the decision to them whether they came in dead or alive. He hired out once or twice in his youth to actually kill a man, but had never acquired a taste for it and soon gave it up. He saved his killing for men who were trying to kill him.

"Here ya go," the barkeep said, putting a mug in front of him.

"Thanks." He dug in his pocket for a coin.

"You're Locke, right?" the man asked.

"That's right."

The bartender showed his palm and said, "Beer's on the house."

"Thanks."

"Just give me a wave when you want another."

"One's my limit."

"It's a smart man who knows his limit," the bartender said, "and I ain't met too many smart men in my time behind the stick. The name's Ames, Ben Ames."

The barkeep stuck out his hand and Locke shook it briefly. Long handshakes were not something he felt comfortable with. They tied up his gun hand for too long.

"You're gonna have a time of it getting Colon strung up, you know," Ames said.

"So I understand."

"Ain't gonna get much help from the sheriff, either."

"That a fact?"

"Oh, yeah," Ames said, leaning his elbows on the bar to talk while Locke worked on his beer. He looked to be a few years younger than Locke, and apparently had the mileage to talk. "His boys ain't gonna want to lose him, not while there's still money to be made from him."

"You know any of his boys?"

"By sight," Ames said.

"Any in here?"

"If there were you'd end up shootin' up my place," the man said, "but no, there ain't. They're lyin' low, I guess, until they can come up with a plan. What about you? Familiar with any of them?"

"Enough to know they're not coming up with a plan

any time soon," Locke said. "They'll be too busy fighting among themselves to see who's in charge now."

"You do know 'em, then," Ames said. "Look, I wasn't always a stick man and saloon owner. You need any help you let me know. I can handle a shotgun."

"Why would you want to do that?" Locke asked, working his beer down below half full.

"Two reasons," Ames said. "One, this town is my home, now. It's where I picked to settle, and I don't want it gettin' shot up."

"And two?"

Ames straightened up, wiped at the bar with a rag and said, "I get bored standin' behind here for too long."

Locke finished his beer off in two big swallows and said, "Ben, I'll keep that in mind."

SIXTEEN

Carlos Mendoza wiped the sleep from his eyes and poured himself a cup of coffee. He set the pot onto the campfire and rocked back on his heels. This was not an easy position for him to be in, for he was a very tall man. He did not, however, want to get too comfortable, and in this position he could spring to his feet at a moment's notice.

Behind him he could hear the others waking—stretching, coughing, spitting. He wondered if his ongoing argument with Francisco Razo over who should be the leader of Ignacio Colon's gang had resulted in Ignacio's death. No, they had a man in Fredericksburg to tell them when the hanging was scheduled, and that had not yet happened.

Mendoza wondered if he should just let Razo take over. After all, they had only to free Ignacio and then he would be back in charge again. The problem, however, was that Mendoza thought Razo was an idiot. The man had a reputation as a hotheaded killer, which did not make him a good choice as leader. Mendoza had killed his share of men, but he did not enjoy it the way Razo did. Mendoza considered himself to have leadership qualities, but in order to get the men to follow him he was going to have to prove himself.

He dumped the remnants of his coffee into the fire and looked over his shoulder again. About half the men had stirred, and half of those were on their feet. Razo, however, was still fast asleep with his sombrero over his eyes. This was further proof that the man was not a leader. The top man in any gang should awaken first, as an example to his men, as Mendoza did each morning.

"Buenos días, Carlos," Hernando Juarez greeted him as he approached the fire.

Mendoza, at thirty-eight, was the oldest of the fifteen men in the gang. Older by several years than Ignacio Colon, himself. Juarez, his staunchest supporter, was thirty. Razo and the others were all under thirty—which in Mendoza's mind was another point against Francisco Razo. However, some of the younger men in the gang were supporting him because he was their age.

Juarez poured himself some coffee and scratched his belly, pulling his shirt up to get at it.

"Have you decided what to do today?" he asked. "I mean, what argument you will make—"

"No more arguments, Hernando."

"What? You will give the leadership to Francisco?" Juarez asked, shocked.

"I did not say that," Mendoza replied. "I said no more arguments. I have decided that a leader must do less talking, and take action."

"And today you will take action?"

Mendoza looked at Juarez and said, "I will take action now."

"But wha——" Juarez started to ask, but it was too late.

Mendoza stood up, turned, walked over to where Francisco Razo was lying, still asleep. Some of the men who had risen greeted him, but he ignored them. He drew his gun, pointed it at Razo's sombrero and fired two shots. The sombrero jumped, but settled back in place over Razo's face. Slowly, the hat began to turn red as blood soaked into it. Mendoza ejected the two spent shells from his Colt and replaced them with two live rounds before turning to face the men.

The ones who were awake stood staring at him in shock. Those who had been awakened by the two shots were scrambling to their feet, looking around them wildly, trying to figure out what had happened.

"Francisco Razo is dead," Mendoza announced.

Gradually, all of the men figured out what had occurred and were looking at him. Off to one side Hernando Juarez stood with his hands on both his guns, in case Mendoza needed someone to back him up.

Mendoza waved his gun and announced, "I am now the leader. I will now decide when and how we will go to Fredericksburg to rescue Ignacio Colon, our rightful leader."

He gave them time to take this in. Some of them went over to where Razo was lying, and one of them even leaned over and took a quick peek underneath the sombrero. He reported to the others that Francisco Razo was indeed dead, shot neatly through each eye. This had been

Mendoza's plan, and he was pleased he had pulled it off. It meant that he was taking over with style. Ignacio would like that when he returned.

"Now you must all ask yourselves if you object," he went on. "If you do, step up now and say so. We will settle the objections here and now. There will be no more talk about this. Our beloved Ignacio has been in a jail cell far too long, and the hangman's noose grows nearer and nearer."

He looked over at Juarez, who simply nodded. Naturally, Hernando Juarez would be the number two man and upon Ignacio Colon's return Mendoza would speak to the leader about promoting the man.

For now he faced the others and said, "So? Anyone?"

There were no takers. In death Francisco Razo had lost all his supporters. Mendoza holstered his gun.

"Then go now. Bury Francisco, and when you finish I will tell you how we will break Ignacio Colon out of the gringo jail."

SEVENTEEN

Locke woke the next morning at 6 A.M. with a clear head. One beer will do that for you. He dressed, putting on yesterday's shirt, but taking a clean shirt down to the lobby with him and arranging for a bath. After the bath he dressed in the clean shirt—this one brown, not blue— and then went back to the lobby.

"Is there anyplace I can get a shirt cleaned?" he asked. He only had the two.

"We got a chink's down the street that'll clean it for ya," the clerk said.

"Could you have somebody take it over there for me? And then put it back in my room when it's clean."

"Yessir, Mr. Locke. No problem at all."

"Thank you."

He stepped outside and although it was not yet 8 A.M. the sun was out in full force and the heat was already oppressive. He returned to the first café he'd eaten at when he got to town because it was good enough for an edible steak-and-egg breakfast. After that he'd have to go and figure out what date to tell Nina Ballinger to put on the invitations. To that end he thought the first person he should talk to was the guest of honor himself, Ignacio Colon.

The sheriff let him in to see Colon without comment. Apparently, he had received his instructions from the council to cooperate every step of the way.

"By the way, Sheriff," he said, before entering the cell block, "I heard tell around town about your new method for capturing deadly bandidos."

"Wha——" the sheriff said, but Locke entered and pulled the door shut himself, cutting the man off. Let him think it over for a while.

Colon was still the only guest in the house, and he smiled his golden smile when he saw who his visitor was.

"Ah, Señor Locke. What a pleasure to see you again. You have come, perhaps, to measure my neck for the hangman's noose?"

"Not my job, Ignacio, but I'll see that it gets done by someone who knows what he's doing. We wouldn't want your neck to survive the fall without breaking. Strangling to death at the end of the noose is a messy way to go."

"Gracias, Señor Locke," Colon said. "Your concern for my well-being does my heart good."

"I just want to see to it that you make it to the gallows in one piece, Ignacio."

"My men will make sure that does not happen."

"Seems to me your men have left you here pretty long already," Locke said. "Maybe they've given up on you?"

Colon chuckled and said, "That is not likely."

"You still got Mendoza and Razo riding with you?" Locke asked.

"Perhaps."

"From what I've heard about those two seems they don't get along. Might take them some time to come up with a plan. First they'll have to fight over who the new leader will be."

"Sí, that will happen," Colon said, "but I suspect by now that Carlos has emerged victorious and is planning my escape even as we speak."

"Why do you assume Mendoza will win out?"

"Razo is not a leader, señor," Colon said. "He wants to be, but alas, he is not. By now I fear he is dead, for Carlos will not argue very long before he takes action."

"And he'll kill Razo to assume command?"

The bandit leader gave Locke the full effect of his golden smile. "But of course."

"Survival of the fittest, eh?"

"No, señor," Colon said, "of the smartest."

It was fortunate that Colon was arrogant and liked to talk. If his assumptions were right Locke had to get the invitations out as soon as possible, and that meant setting a date for the hanging. He also needed a carpenter to construct the gallows. And they were going to need a hangman, and a doctor.

The sheriff glared at him as he let Locke out of the cell block.

"You know, I caught Colon fair and square," he said, sullenly.

"So I heard," Locke said, "if tripping over him was fair and square."

"Ain't my fault his horse threw him."

"Sheriff, how many deputies you got?"

"Full time, two."

"How many more can you get?"

"Depends on who volunteers."

"What's the largest posse you've ever put together?"

"That'd be the one that went out after Colon and his men," the lawman said. "Ten men."

"Ten?"

"That's right."

"And how many men did Colon have?"

"I don't know," the man said. "Fourteen or fifteen."

"And they ran from your posse?"

"We was duly appointed—" Sheriff Horrigan was saying, but Locke stopped listening. Something wasn't right here. Why would Colon and his men run from a posse of ten men—if Horrigan was even telling the truth—led by an inexperienced sheriff? And how could such a man capture a famous bandido by tripping over him?

He left Horrigan still trying to defend himself and his posse.

EIGHTEEN

Locke went directly to Gordon Vestal's store from the jail. He probably should have gone to find the judge, but he had a feeling he could handle everything through Vestal. He knew what he needed in order to figure out when to hang Colon. He just needed to get it all settled so he could have Nina print out the invitations. He was hoping that he wouldn't have to spend too long in Fredericksburg. He wanted to get Colon hung and then get back north, where it might be a bit cooler.

"Good morning," Vestal said, as Locke entered. The store was empty for the moment, which suited Locke.

"Vestal, I need to set a date for the hanging."

"Set it, then," Vestal said. "We'll do it whenever you say."

"I'll need to talk to a carpenter first, about constructing the gallows. Is there one in town?"

"A very fine one. He built an extension onto this building. His name is Gavin James and he has a workshop at the south end of the main street, across from Johnson's Livery Stable." Vestal frowned. "Isn't that where you put your horse up?"

"As a matter of fact, it is," Locke said, "and I seem to remember the carpenter across the way. I'll go and talk to him right now."

"How are your invitations coming? Is Nina . . . obliging you?"

Locke studied Vestal for any sign of a double meaning in his words.

"She's waiting for me to give her the date. I notice that some of the names on the list of victims' families—many of them, in fact—don't have addresses where they can get regular mail. I'm going to need some men to hand deliver quite a few of them."

"I can get you some men," Vestal said. "Just tell me how many."

"Two should do it."

"I'll have them present themselves to you at your hotel."

"That's fine."

"Anything else?"

"Not at the moment."

Locke did have more questions, but he wasn't ready to ask them of the storeowner just then.

"Well, let me know."

Locke turned to leave, then stopped short.

"There is one other thing."

"What's that?"

"Where can I get ahold of Judge Tinsley if I need him?"

"Either at the courthouse—the City Hall building—or at his home. He lives in a house at the north end of town. He's pretty much at one of those three places, unless he's eating, and he takes all his meals at, uh, The Dexter

House, where we saw you last night. How did you like the food, by the way?"

"The steak was very good."

"You and Nina seemed to be getting on well."

"As you said, she's cooperating."

"Mmm. I have not found Nina Ballinger to be a very cooperative person."

"Maybe you just haven't given her a chance," Locke said. "Now that she's a member of the board—"

"Actually," Vestal said, interrupting Locke as gingerly as he could, "she hasn't officially accepted the position yet."

"Oh," Locke said, "I'm sure she will, and I'm sure she'll be an asset to your council, and to the town. She seems to be a very intelligent woman."

"Mmm," Vestal said, again, "yes, no one ever said she wasn't intelligent."

"Well," Locke said, "I'll go and talk with Mr. James. Thanks for the information."

As Locke left, Gordon Vestal frowned and rubbed his jaw. He hoped that hiring John Locke was not going to turn out to backfire.

NINETEEN

As Locke approached the carpentry he remembered seeing it when he had first ridden into town, but never expected he'd have occasion to visit it.

He opened the front door and entered, breathing in the scent of fresh cut wood. The room had a high ceiling and looked like a warehouse rather than a workshop. Banging was coming from somewhere in the back and he followed the noise. He found a man working in a small area, on something that appeared to be a piece of furniture. He waited for a lull before he spoke.

"Gavin James?"

The man holding the hammer looked up jerkily, startled. He gripped the hammer harder when he saw Locke.

"Can I help you?" he demanded, almost belligerently.

"I hope so. My name is John Locke."

Suddenly, James's grip on the hammer loosened.

He put the hammer down and approached Locke, extending his hand. "It's good to meet you. I hear you're gonna make sure that bastard Colon gets strung up good and proper."

"I'm going to do my best, but I'll need your help."

"My help? For what?"

"The gallows."

"Ah." James was in his early thirties, a large, strapping man with heavy calluses on his hands. Locke had felt them when they shook.

"Can you handle a job that big?"

"See this place?" James asked.

"Yes."

"I built this. All of it. I keep a lot of supplies on hand."

"Enough to build a gallows?"

"Plenty."

"The job's yours if you want it."

James frowned. "My understanding is that you are to have whatever you want, no charge. Does that include the gallows?"

"No," Locke said. "I'll make sure you get paid for your work."

"Then I accept the job," James said, and the two men shook hands again.

"I'll need you to stop whatever you're doing now and start immediately. And I need to know how long it will take."

"I can let you know tomorrow, if that's all right?"

"The sooner the better," Locke said. "Sometime today would be good, but tomorrow at the latest. I have to send out invitations."

"To a hanging?"

"There are family members who should be present," Locke said. "Family of the people Colon and his men have killed."

"I understand," James said. "They'll want to see him swing."

"Exactly. In fact . . . I think we'll need someplace to put them so they can get a good view."

"I know what you mean," James said. "The street will be mobbed for this. I could build you a small viewing stand, high up, but not as high as the gallows. Just enough so they can see over the heads of the crowd."

"That's a great idea," Locke said. "Do it."

"All right," the carpenter said, "I'll let you know as soon as I can how long I'll need."

"I appreciate that. Oh, you couldn't build a coffin, too, could you?"

"Nope, I don't do that kind of work," James said. "There's a coffin maker in town, works closely with the undertaker."

"I guess I'll have to see them, too."

"A lot of work, planning a hanging, isn't it?"

"Apparently."

"A rope and a tree," James said. "That's the way they used to do it. At least, that's what I heard when I was growing up back East."

"A rope and a tree used to be the way," Locke said, "but in a much simpler time."

TWENTY

Locke decided to write down everything he had to do. He stopped at his hotel, procured a piece of paper and a pencil from the young clerk, and took them out to the porch with him to make his list. His clean shirt was already soaked through with sweat, so this would give him time to dry off, as well.

Date.
Invitations.
Gallows.
Doctor.
Undertaker.
Coffin maker.

Once the carpenter let him know how much time he needed he'd be able to set a date. There was nothing he could do about that now. He could, however, go to the newspaper office and let Nina Ballinger know what was going on. After that he'd go and talk to the undertaker, the coffin maker, and the local doctor.

He went back inside, returned the pencil to the clerk,

and stuffed the piece of paper in his pocket. After that he left the hotel and walked to the newspaper office.

He walked through the clatter of the press again and knocked on Nina Ballinger's door. Just walking from the hotel to here his shirt was stuck to his back again. There was no way around this, it was just too damn hot.

Whether she heard the knock or not she spotted him when turning around and waved him in.

"For a man who's not interested in women we're seeing quite a bit of each other," she said, and immediately colored as if she regretted the statement. She needn't have, since he ignored it.

"Do you have the date for the hanging?" she asked, hurriedly.

"Not yet," he said, "but I should have it either tonight or tomorrow."

"All right, then," she said. "I'll put the invitations aside until tomorrow. Thanks for letting me know."

"You're welcome."

"Now, about the interview—"

"Tomorrow," he said, "after the invitations have been printed."

"Shall we do it over dinner, then?"

"Why not?" he asked. "You should know, however, that having dinner with me sort of puts a lot of attention on you."

"Maybe," she said, "having dinner with me puts attention on you. Did you ever think of that?"

* * *

He left the office of the *Front Page* after obtaining directions from Nina Ballinger to the undertaker's, the doctor's, and the coffin maker's. The doctor's office was the closest.

"I know who you are, Mr. Locke," Doctor Emmett Stone said as they shook hands. "I've been advised, like everyone else in town, to give you all the assistance I can."

"I appreciate that, Doctor."

Stone was in his sixties, but there was nothing frail about the man, especially not his handshake, which was firm and strong. He was tall, still sturdily built, and his blue eyes were clear and steady.

"What can I do for you?"

"Well, it's very simple, actually," Locke said. "It's my job to make sure that everything goes smoothly with this hanging. I'll just need you to pronounce the prisoner dead after it's over."

"I can do that very easily," Doctor Stone said, "and, I might add, gladly."

"Why gladly?"

"Because I've had many of Ignacio Colon's victims brought here to me with bullet holes in them—holes that I couldn't patch up in time to save most of their lives. I can't wait to see the man fall through the trapdoor of the gallows. That will be justice."

"No argument here, Doctor."

Next he went to see the undertaker. He was quite surprised to find Ned Bates to be a positively cherubic looking man. In his forties and barely five foot five, Bates's cheeks were like two ripe apples.

"A pleasure to make your acquaintance, sir," the man said, shaking Locke's hand vigorously. "A pleasure. Whatever I can do for you will be my pleasure."

"Your part will be probably the simplest of all, Mr. Bates," Locke said, wondering why an undertaker would use the word *pleasure* so much. Also, he noticed a sour smell in the air, but decided not to dwell on what might be the cause of it. "You just have to bury the man."

"It's never quite as simple as that, is it, sir?" Bates asked. "No, there's much more to it than that. People don't understand just what a burial entails. Why, there are all sorts of things to be decided. The type of funeral, what kind of coffin, the viewing—"

"Just bury him, Mr. Bates," Locke said, "the simplest, easiest, fastest, cheapest way you know how."

"Cheap?"

"Well," Locke said, suddenly changing his mind, "the town will pay you for your time, so why don't you give him the grandest send-off you can think of?"

"Really?" the man asked. Locke didn't think his cheeks could grow any rosier, but they were. He was positively gleeful.

"Sure, why not?" Locke added. "Every man deserves a send-off, don't they?"

"I believe so," Ned Bates said. "In fact, my sainted father used to say exactly the same thing. He started this business, you know."

"Nice of you to follow in your father's footsteps,

Mr. Bates," Locke said. "Now I just need to go and talk to the coffin maker."

"Frank Barlow," Bates said. "Just down the street. Does marvelous work. Tell him we discussed his top-of-the-line coffin."

"I'll do that, Mr. Bates," Locke said, "I'll surely do that."

Locke left, wishing he could see the faces of the Town Council members when they got the bill for the funeral of Ignacio Colon.

In appearance, Frank Barlow ran true to form. He looked more like an undertaker than the undertaker did, a very slender man with a baleful expression and jug-handled ears. Locke wondered if his was also a business handed down to him by his father?

Once again Locke shook hands with a stranger. He couldn't remember the last time he'd done that so much during the course of one day.

"Would you like to see what I have?" the coffin maker asked. "I can take you into my workshop."

The smell in the air there was almost the same as at the carpenter's, just not as fresh or overpowering. And it was much better than the smell at the undertaker's.

"That won't be necessary," Locke said. "I've already spoken with Mr. Bates and we've decided that we need your top-of-the-line box."

"Ah, excellent choice," Barlow said, "but, um, the cost—"

"—will be covered by the Town Council," Locke assured him. "Just send them the bill. In fact, why don't you send it right to Judge Tinsley?"

"Judge Tinsley?"

"Is that a problem?"

"No, it's just . . ." Barlow paused and looked around, then said in a low voice, ". . . the judge didn't go top-of-the-line when his own wife died."

"Well, Mr. Barlow," Locke said, "maybe this will be his way of making up for it."

Earlier that day the man had taken up position across the street from the undertaker's. From that vantage point he was also able to keep the coffin maker's place in sight. He thought this would be better than trying to follow a man like John Locke around town. With his reputation preceding him, that would have been a sure way to let Locke know he was being watched. Anticipating where he might go and then getting there first, that was the smart thing to do.

Once Locke had come out of the newspaper office without the invitations the man knew that the date of the hanging had not yet been set. But since Locke was going through the motions of getting everything in order, the date figured to be not too far away.

Suddenly, an idea occurred to the man and he realized he didn't have to follow Locke, or anticipate his moves.

There was another way.

TWENTY-ONE

Locke left the coffin maker's shop and mentally ticked off the stops on his list. What else was there to do that he hadn't written down? He had a sudden urge for coffee so he crossed the street to a café that was handy and went inside. As he did he caught sight of a man stepping out of the café and walking off down the street. There was something familiar about him, but he hadn't gotten a good enough look.

As he entered, the place was empty, so he had the choice of tables and took one in the back. A bored-looking woman in her forties came out and asked him what he wanted.

"Just coffee," he said.

"Only customer all day and all you want is coffee?" she asked. "And on a hot day like this?"

"If that's all right with you," he said.

"Fine."

She turned and walked away and he was glad he hadn't decided to order something to eat. If the townspeople avoided this place there must have been a good reason for it.

The reason became apparent when she came back with the coffee.

To get rid of the bad taste lingering in his mouth Locke decided to have his one beer early that day. He started in the direction of his hotel and stopped at the first saloon he came to. Coincidentally, it was the Whiskey and Gambling place he'd been in before. Ben Ames was either still behind the bar, or behind it again.

"Back so soon?" he asked. "Couldn't stay away, huh?"

"I think I just had the worst coffee in town," Locke said.

"Well, my beer is the cure fir what ails you," Ames said.

"Prove it."

Ames went and drew a cold one and brought it over.

"Go ahead," Ames said. "It's on the house."

The beer would have been on the house anyway, but Locke knew what he meant. He took a healthy sip, then found himself gulping down half of it. When he came up for air the taste of the bad coffee was completely gone.

"That do it for ya?" Ames asked.

"Yeah, that did it, all right," Locke said. "Thanks."

"How are plans for the hanging going?" Ames asked, dropping his bartender's elbows down onto the bar.

"Slowly, at first," Locke said, "but things may be picking up."

Normally a reticent man at best, Locke often found himself able to talk with bartenders. For one thing, they were people he probably would see a few times, and then never again. Secondly, they were used to listening to people's troubles and travails, and then forgetting them. However, this was also one of the reasons Locke did not drink a lot when working. There was one time, back when he first gave up the marshal's position in Tombstone, when he'd stood at a bar all night drinking and complaining to the bartender, and the next morning he'd woken up in bed with a whore. He had full memory of everything he said and did the night before and he swore not only to never see that bartender again, but never to go into that saloon again. After that he monitored his drinking and chose carefully the nights he was going to overindulge.

He looked down at the beer that remained in his mug and made sure that it took him twice as long to finish it as the first half. Sometimes, the stuff just went down too damn easy.

TWENTY-TWO

ocke was on his third beer when he realized he'd gone past his first. Then he was on the fifth and didn't remember having his second.

"You all right?" Ben Ames asked.

Locke squinted across the bar at Ames.

"I'm fine," he said. "I just realized something."

"What?"

"Never mind," Locke said. "It's private."

"Hey, friend," Ames said. "I'm a bartender, remember? You can tell me anything."

Locke stared at Ames and knew that if he had one more drink he would be telling the bartender anything that came into his head.

"Gotta go," he said.

"Come back soon," Ames said as Locke pushed away from the bar. "And remember my offer."

Locke waved and went out through the bat-wing doors, bumping into two men as they were coming in.

"Hey!" one of them shouted. "Watch where you're goin'!"

Locke stopped, turned, and faced both men.

"You talking to me?" he asked.

The two men looked Locke up and down and when they got to his eyes they froze.

"Uh, hey, no harm done, friend," one of them said. The other man just waved no.

Locke felt something welling up from inside of him, and knew that if he let it free he'd have a hell of a time getting it back down again.

"Just watch it next time," he growled at them.

"Sure, sure," the men said.

As Locke watched them walk away he heard one of the men say, "Damn drunk."

When Locke reached his hotel he didn't bother stepping up onto the porch, he just sat down on the front steps. His mind took him back to Tombstone, back to the night he faced down the three men who had tried to rob the poker game at the Bird Cage. . . .

He'd had more than one beer that night, and he didn't always remember all the details the same way every time he thought about it. Today, however, he remembered that he'd fired four shots, not three. He'd taken out the two standing men, and then gave the third man a chance to draw. If he hadn't been drunk he might have simply brought the man in, given him a chance to give up. But he didn't, he faced him down and shot him dead, and he fired twice at the man, not once. That second shot had killed a man standing behind him, one of the other poker players.

An innocent bystander . . .

* * *

"We're here to decide whether or not John Locke should continue to hold the position as marshal of Tombstone. In light of the fact that he's killed some ten men since he took office, one of them by accident because he'd been drinking—"

"All but one in the line of duty," one member of the council felt bound to point out. He was the only member who intended to vote no to stripping Locke of his badge, but all the others were in favor of it.

"That may be true," Newberry said, *"but there might have been other ways to get the job done . . . because of the incidents that took place in the Bird Cage several nights ago I think it's time to call for a vote. All those in favor—"*

"I'll save you the trouble, Ted," Locke said. . . .

A voice called his name, bringing him back to the present.

"What?" He looked up.

"I figured out how long it will take me to build the gallows," Gavin James, the carpenter, said.

"Hmm?"

"The gallows?"

Locke shook his head hard enough to shake the past from it, but not hard enough to completely dispel the fog. . . .

"Oh, carpenter," he said.

"No, Gavin James."

"Yes," Locke said, "but you're the carpenter . . ."

"Oh, right."

Locke cleared his throat, and spat into the street.

"All right," he said, "how long?"

"I can do it in three days, but I'll need to hire two helpers, and we'll have to work long hours."

"Two days?"

"Quickest I can do it. We've got to dig holes for the posts, construct the platform. I don't have the trapdoor mechanism usually needed, but I can rig something—"

"No, no," Locke said, waving his hand, "there's no need to explain. I just needed a number."

"Two days," James said, nodding.

Locke frowned, concentrating.

"That's with the viewing stand?"

"Yes."

"Tomorrow's Wednesday?"

"That's right."

Locke rubbed his face vigorously.

"Are you all right, Mr. Locke?" James asked. "Can I . . . do anything for you?"

"No, no," Locke said, "I'm fine, just fine." He paused a moment, trying to concentrate. "All right, then, we'll hang him on Saturday."

"And I'll get myself two men and get started as early in the morning as I can," Gavin James said. "Luckily I have what I need in the shop. See you tomorrow."

"Right," Locke said, and as the carpenter walked away he added, "Yeah, it's lucky. . . ."

He watched the carpenter walk away, then stood up slowly and carefully. There was a day when he could drink half a dozen beers and not feel a thing, but those days were obviously gone. Tomorrow he'd be back to his one beer a day. This was a momentary setback, but he'd had them before. He could control it. He could always control it. . . .

TWENTY-THREE

When Locke woke the next morning his head was pounding and his mouth felt dry, his tongue thick. He'd done it again, he realized. He sat on the end of the bed with his head in his hands, wondering why he had wasted a good six months in one night. Six months, and never a day with more than one drink. That had been his personal record, but he'd shot it to hell last night, and he didn't even know why. There was nothing he could figure that could have triggered it. All he remembered was the desire to get a bad taste out of his mouth. What a stupid reason to throw away six months of self-control.

He stood up and dressed slowly. He knew what he had to do. He needed a long bath, and some breakfast—even though that would make two baths in two days. He usually saved that kind of behavior for trips to San Francisco. Out here in the West two in two days was rare, but more than a bath he needed a good long soak . . . a cleansing. . . .

He put on the same shirt he'd worn the day before, even though his other shirt had been cleaned and returned. In his pocket he found his list. He hunted around the room until he found a pencil, and then drew a line through each task he'd completed. He couldn't think of anything else to do until he got his head clear.

He went downstairs to arrange for a bath.

After he'd had a long bath Locke went to the café he had come to think of as reliable, if not good. He had a large breakfast, including a pot of coffee which, in comparison to the cup he'd had the night before, was excellent.

It was during breakfast that he remembered Gavin James speaking to him on the front porch, but for the life of him he could not remember what was said. Surely it had to do with constructing the gallows. He was going to have to visit the carpenter and see if he could find out what they had talked about, without letting on that he couldn't recall.

He took out his list again and studied it. He'd crossed everything off except the invitations themselves, which meant he'd had a productive day yesterday. Why, then, had he jeopardized his own success? He decided not to ponder the question too long, because whenever he did he was always left feeling frustrated. Better to get back to work than try to struggle with an answer that would not come.

He paid for his breakfast and left the café, heading for the carpenter's workshop.

TWENTY-FOUR

As he entered he was greeted by the sounds of hammering and sawing. Apparently, work had already begun. He walked toward the sounds and found Gavin James and another man hard at it. He had to wait for the banging to stop before announcing himself.

"Mr. James!"

The carpenter looked at Locke and smiled. The other man paused in his work to watch. They had both removed their shirts, as the heat inside was as oppressive as it was outside. Their torsos had sweat positively sluicing off them.

"Just call me Gavin," James said, "and this is Henry."

"Howdy," Henry said. He was a big, powerfully built man who looked as if he could erect a gallows with only his two bare hands.

"He's one of the two men I told you I'd need to get this finished in time for your hanging on Saturday."

And there it was, and he didn't even have to ask.

"That's good."

"You're looking better this morning," James said. "Are you all right?"

"I'm fine," Locke said. "What about the other man?"

"I sent him out for some things. He's probably at Gordon Vestal's store right now."

Locke nodded, then said, "Could we talk outside a moment?"

"Sure." James put his hammer down. "Keep at it, Henry."

"Sure thing."

James followed Locke outside, closing the front door behind him. Locke could still hear the pounding.

"Where'd you get these two men?" he asked.

"I use Henry whenever I need another hand—or two," James said, with a smile.

"And the other one?"

"He was looking for work."

"You don't know him?"

"Met him yesterday, after I left you."

"So he's not from around here?"

"No. Is that a problem?"

"No, no," Locke said, "I'm just asking. . . . Is he experienced?"

"Not like Henry, but he'll do."

"What's his name?"

"Umm, Dan . . . something . . . Callahan, I think. Maybe Carter? Why don't you come by and meet him later?"

"Okay," Locke said, "all right. I'll do that. I'll let you get back to work now."

"We've been at it for hours already," Gavin James said. "We'll be ready."

Locke nodded and said, "Thanks."

As Locke was walking down the main street toward the center of town he suddenly realized what was missing from his list.

"Goddamnit!" He'd have to stop and see the judge about it, but first he wanted to give Nina Ballinger the date of the hanging.

"That's short notice," she said, then added, "not that the town won't turn out. They've been waiting for this for a long time. Once you post it—"

"Post it?"

"Well, you are going to post the date around town, aren't you? I assumed you'd want some fliers?"

"Oh, yeah, sure," Locke said, "that's right." Something else he'd forgotten, but then he'd never hosted a hanging before.

"I can print up fliers with the same information as the invitations. I know a couple of boys who will hang them up for two bits each," she said. "They're good kids."

"That'll be fine."

"And I'll get these invitations printed right away. You can pick everything up in about two hours."

"Thank you, Miss Ballinger."

She cocked her head to one side and asked, "Can I get you to call me Nina?"

He hesitated.

"No strings attached," she said. "It's just easier, and I prefer the informality."

He felt the opposite way, but gave in. "All right, then . . . Nina."

"And can I call you John? I mean, since I'll be interviewing you later this evening."

"Sure, that's fine."

"You seem distracted today, John. Is there some problem?"

"No," he said, "nothing serious. I . . . had a bad night."

"Did you drink too much?" she asked, laughing.

"Why do you ask that?" he snapped.

"Hey," she said, "I was just kidding."

"Oh, well . . . uh, no, I just . . . didn't sleep well, is all. I'll be back in a couple of hours. Thanks . . . Nina."

"You're welcome," she said, "but don't worry, I'll get my recompense this evening."

"This evening," he said, "right."

"Over dinner, remember?"

"Yes," he said, "I do remember. Can we make it tomorrow? You choose the place and the Town Council will buy dinner."

"You have a date," she said, and then stammered, "I mean—uh, not a real date—it was just a figure of speech. . . ."

He thought she was a little old to be that flustered, but said, "I'll see you later," and left.

TWENTY-FIVE

Locke found Judge Tinsley in his office at the courthouse, which was in the City Hall building. He was seated behind a large, pitted, solid oak desk that fit him perfectly.

"Mr. Locke," the older man said, waving. "Come in, come in. How are things going?"

"Pretty good, Judge," Locke said. "I've set Saturday for the date of the hanging."

"So soon?"

"Well, Colon has been a prisoner for some time now and his men are bound to come after him," Locke said. "Now that I'm in charge I'd like to get it over with. Why? Is that a problem?"

"A problem? No, not at all," the judge said. "Why would that be a problem?"

"I didn't think it would be," Locke said. "Mr. Vestal is supplying me with men to hand deliver the invitations to the family members."

"Excellent, excellent."

"And I'm having some fliers posted around town so that everybody knows about it."

"Good idea."

Judge Tinsley's attitude belied his words, though. Something seemed to be bothering him.

"Judge? We don't have any problems here, do we?" Maybe he'd heard about last night, maybe another Town Council was going to fire him. Maybe—

"There's nothing wrong, Mr. Locke," the judge said, "I assure you. I'm happy to hear that you have a schedule."

"Yes, I do," Locke said, "and I intend to keep it. I've got someone building the gallows, and it will be ready in time. And I've spoken with the doctor, the undertaker, and the coffin maker."

"You have been busy, indeed," Tinsley said. "It looks like we may have hired the right man for the job."

"There's just one other thing I need and then all the arrangements will be made."

"And what is that?"

"A hangman."

"I'm sorry, I thought you said—"

"An executioner," Locke said, "someone to pull the lever when the time comes."

"Well . . . I thought that would be you."

Locke shook his head.

"I don't mind being a host, Judge," he said, "a master of ceremonies, but I draw the line at being the hangman. We need a professional, and he has two days to get here."

"I see."

"I thought you might know someone. . . ."

"Well, I do, but I don't think he can get here in time to, uh, officiate."

"What about you, then?"

"Me?" the judge seemed taken aback by the suggestion. "I'm afraid I'm no more a hangman than you are, sir."

"Okay, then I think I know somebody who can get here in time, but he won't come cheap."

"A friend of yours?"

"Yes."

"Get him, then," the judge said. "We'll pay him. It would be worth almost anything to get this over with."

"I'll send a telegram today," Locke said. "He lives in New Mexico. Unless he's away on another job I'm sure he'll be able to get here."

"And who is this gentleman?"

"His name is Arlo Hawkes."

"Hawkes!" Tinsley said. "I know that name."

"Yes, he has a reputation."

"With a gun, if I'm not mistaken."

"That may be," Locke said, "but his business is hanging men, not shooting them."

"Yes," the judge said, "I seem to remember that about him, too."

"Shall I get him?"

The judge sighed and said, "If you can, but I want no gunplay in town, Locke."

"Judge," Locke said, "if you were afraid of gunplay I don't think you would have hired me."

As Locke left City Hall in search of the telegraph office he replayed the scene with the judge in his head. The man was hiding something, and he realized now that he was getting the same feeling about Gordon Vestal. He wasn't being told everything. Before this was over he'd find out what was being kept from him.

He sent off a telegram to Arlo Hawkes in White Oaks, New Mexico. Hawkes had been scheduled to be the man to hang Billy the Kid when the Kid escaped and was later shot and killed by Pat Garrett in Fort Sumner. During that time, though, Hawkes had come to like Lincoln County in general, and White Oaks in particular. Locke told the telegraph operator to bring the reply to his hotel, and leave it with the hotel clerk if he wasn't there.

Locke had not seen Doc Holliday since he left Tombstone, but he still counted Doc as his best friend. After Doc, though, would come Arlo Hawkes. The only problem with hanging around Hawkes was that the man was a hard drinker, and it never seemed to faze him. He knew about Locke's battles with his particular demons, but Hawkes was of the opinion that a man fought those battles alone. So he drank the same way, whether he was around Locke or not.

But having Hawkes's gun in town would be worth the temptation to drink with him. Ignacio Colon's men were sure to try and break him out. It might even be easier for them to take him right from the gallows, when he'd be out in the open, eliminate the need to get inside the jail.

It would be good to see Hawkes again. It had been a while since Locke had spent time with a man he really liked and respected. This late in life, after Tombstone and with the drinking, he didn't have much patience for people—and not a lot for himself, either.

He decided to go ahead back to the hotel, recalling that Vestal was going to send over a couple of men to deliver the invitations. If that was the case he'd send one of them to the newspaper office to pick the invitations up while he remained at the hotel, waiting for a reply from Arlo Hawkes.

TWENTY-SIX

Ignacio Colon had chosen a not quite box canyon dangerously close to town for him and his men to hide out in. It would have been a box except that there were two ways in and out. There was a small herd of wild ponies there when they arrived but they drove them out and made themselves at home. After he was captured, his men returned to the canyon, for want of someplace better to go. The herd of ponies was there again, but this time the bandits left them alone. They took one side of the canyon while the horses inhabited the other side. Oddly, the smell of the men and the campfire did not seem to spook the animals.

Carlos Mendoza stood staring out at the horses, thinking about Colon. They had met as young men in their teens, on equal terms, but after that first day they were never equals again. From that time on Mendoza had followed Colon, been his second no matter who else was around. For Francisco Razo to have aspired to that number two role was ridiculous—but not as ridiculous as his wanting to be leader. He had managed to convince some of the younger bandidos of his worthiness to lead, but

Mendoza had effectively dispelled that with two well-placed shots. Those men now knew it was obey, or die.

"Carlos."

He turned to find Hernando Juarez approaching him. The man had only been riding with Colon's band for six months, but he had attached himself to Mendoza, and the two men had fought side by side and saved each other's lives many times. If Mendoza had his own outlaw band, Hernando Juarez would be his number two.

"Sí, Hernando?"

"The gringo, he is riding this way. Paolo can see him from the ridge."

They had a man on watch day and night.

"Muy bien," Mendoza said. "He will have the date that has been set for Ignacio's hanging. That is what I have been waiting for."

"So now you will tell us the plan?" Juarez asked.

"Soon enough, Hernando," Mendoza said, "soon enough. Bring the gringo to me when he arrives."

"Sí."

Alone once again Mendoza looked out at the horses. He would tell them the plan when he came up with one. He didn't want anyone to know that he did not yet have one. He had always been very good at carrying out a plan once Ignacio Colon explained it to him. Never before was it necessary for him to come up with one of his own. But he had ridden with Colon for many years now, and watched the man work. He knew how he thought. He felt that he would be able to come up with something worthy of Colon himself.

Eventually.

This time when Juarez approached he had another man with him—the gringo.

"Carlos, he is here."

Mendoza turned and looked at the gringo who was in the employ of Colon. It was this man's job to bring them information about the town, and now he was in Mendoza's employ to bring information about Ignacio Colon's incarceration and execution.

"What have you to tell me?" he demanded.

"The hanging is set for Saturday." The gringo stood nervously, with his hat in his hand.

"So soon? They were not making progress the last time we talked. What has changed?"

"They hired a master of ceremonies."

"A bastonero?" Mendoza asked.

"I've heard that word," the man said. "Yes, that was it."

"And who did they hire?"

"John Locke."

"Locke?"

"You know this man, Carlos?" Juarez asked.

Mendoza frowned.

"If it is the same man," Mendoza said. "There was a man who was the marshal of Tombstone for about six months. They say he ruled with his gun, tamed the town, but was then cast out."

"What happened to him then?"

"I heard he went to Mexico and crawled into a bottle," Mendoza said.

"Well," the gringo said, "looks to me like he crawled out again. That's the man."

"Locke," Juarez said, still frowning. "Why is that name familiar?"

"He is also known as El Viudador."

"Aiee," Juarez said, pointing his finger, "the Widow-maker! I have heard of him! He is deadly with a gun, no?"

"He was deadly with a gun at one time, yes," Mendoza said, "but who knows now?"

"He walks through the town like he owns it," the gringo said. "Everybody's got orders to give him whatever he wants. No way to tell, yet, if he can still handle himself."

"The man may be existing on his reputation," Mendoza said. "This could be good for us."

"How do we find out?" Juarez asked. "How do we find out by Saturday?"

"Ah, a very good question," Mendoza said, "and I think I have the answer."

TWENTY-SEVEN

Locke stared at the beer the hotel bartender had placed before him. Last night he had not been able to stop drinking. This was the test, now, to see if he could go back to one a day.

He took the beer from the bar and carried it with him to a table.

Earlier in the day two men had come to the hotel and found him sitting in the lobby, reading Nina Ballinger's *Fredericksburg Front Page* for that day.

"Mr. Vestal sent us to do some work," one of them said.

Neither man wore a gun. Both were in their twenties, dressed cleanly. Locke wondered if they were clerks in Vestal's store.

One was Ken and the other was Rex. Ken was short, Rex tall, Ken dark haired, Rex fair haired—not that any of that mattered. They would deliver the invitations and he would probably never see them again.

"Go over to the newspaper office and collect the invitations to the hanging of Ignacio Colon. After that you will deliver them to these people." He handed each his own list.

"I don't know where all these places are," Ken said.

"Some are in town, but—" Rex started, but Locke cut him off.

"Hand carry what you can and then ask around about the rest and deliver them," he said. "I want them all delivered by this time tomorrow."

"Mr. Vestal said we'd be paid," Ken said.

"And he'll be the one to pay you," Locke said, "but you'll answer to me if the job's not done. Understand?"

"Yes, sir," Ken said. Rex swallowed and nodded.

"Then go."

Off they went and the invitations were finally on their way. Locke had decided not to check them first. He trusted Nina Ballinger to be efficient. That was how she struck him, efficient and organized. The job would get done.

As for people who were not on the list, the fliers would be distributed throughout the town, nailed to buildings and posts. The date of the hanging had made the front page of the paper. He did not know how far the paper's circulation would take it, but news would get out. It would reach some too late, of course, since the hanging was only three days away, but there was sure to be a good turnout. Soon, the atmosphere would take on the same feeling as when a circus came to town. Ignacio Colon was a famous man, an infamous man, and there were many who would want to see him swing.

Of course, there were a dozen or more who did not.

He remained in the hotel lobby for the rest of the day, where the key operator from the telegraph office found him.

"Your reply, sir."

"Thank you."

He read the telegram. It was typically succinct of Arlo Hawkes. "I'll be there," it said, and Locke knew he'd arrive no later than the day before. He would want to see what he was working with, test the gallows, meet everyone involved.

It was after he read the telegram that he went out to have dinner in his reliable café, and then returned to have his single beer.

Now it sat before him on the table, beads of water sliding down the sides of the mug. He had a headache, and he knew it would go away as soon as he took his first sip. For the first time in months he thought about having a shot of whiskey with it, but he shook his head to dispel the thought. That would be the end of him for a very long time, possibly forever. He did not think he could survive another year like the one he'd endured in that Mexican town, spending day and night drunk out of his mind. But he had come back from that, back to this point, to enjoying one single beer a day. He'd had a setback the night before, but to slide back all the way would probably be a slide back into oblivion.

He was not ready for oblivion. He still had to figure out why the entire Tombstone experience had affected him so. He still didn't understand, after all these years, why giving up that badge had turned him into a drunk, and why the Shootout at the O.K. Corral had sobered him back up.

Oblivion would have to wait until he had figured all of that out.

He picked up the beer, took the first sip, sat back and waited for the pain in his head to go away.

TWENTY-EIGHT

Locke woke the next morning feeling he had accomplished a lot the day before, and not just having to do with the hanging. He was back in control. He was strapping on his gunbelt when there was a knock at his door. With his hand on his gun he answered it.

The man standing in the hall was a stranger. Average height, not wearing a gun, very harmless looking.

"Uh, Mr. Locke?"

"That's right."

"Sir, my name is Dan Callahan. I'm working with Gavin, the carpenter, on constructing the gallows."

"Oh, right," Locke said. He recalled the name. "What can I do for you?"

"Gavin sent me over to ask you the exact location you wanted the gallows and viewing stand set up."

Locke scolded himself. That was something else that should have been on his list.

"Tell Gavin to meet me in front of City Hall in one hour and we'll discuss it."

"Yes, sir, will do." The man hesitated, staring down at Locke's gun.

"Is there something wrong?"

"Huh?" The man tore his eyes from the gun. "Oh, no sir, I'll tell him."

"You do that."

Callahan took off down the hall as Locke stepped out of his room and locked the door.

After breakfast Locke found Gavin James waiting for him in front of City Hall.

"What looks like a likely spot to you?" he asked.

"Right over here. Follow me."

City Hall was situated on Main Street where there was a bend. This created a place off to either side where a scaffold could be erected and not interfere with traffic, the carpenter explained—except, of course, at the actual hangings, when the street would probably be choked with people.

"Fine," Locke said. "Do it."

"Then I thought we'd put the viewing stand over there, next to the City Hall. It will block traffic for a while, but we can erect it last and take it down first."

"Do it," Locke said. "A little traffic jam is a small price to pay."

"You don't have to check with anyone?" the man asked. "The council? the judge?"

"No," Locke said, "I'm in charge of this whole shebang. Start digging your holes."

"Okay," James said. "I, uh, hope you didn't mind me sending Dan over to your room."

"No," Locke said, "I was awake, getting ready to leave, anyway."

"I saw the newspaper yesterday. They didn't waste any time getting the announcement in there."

"Yeah, word will get around now," Locke said. "Attendance should be good."

James shook his head. "Never could understand myself people's eagerness to see a hanging."

"It's morbid, I know," Locke said, "but in this case it's somebody who really deserves it. There'll be a lot of family members of Colon's victims attending. They're entitled to watch him hang, don't you think?"

"I guess," James said. "The whole thing just sounds barbaric to me."

"Well, we could chop off their heads, or have them torn apart by horses."

James shook his head and said, "I mean the whole idea of executions, regardless of the method—but we really shouldn't get involved in discussing that now. I can't really justify my position while I'm building a gallows, can I?"

TWENTY-NINE

Before long the street was filled with the sound of construction as James and his helpers started building the scaffolding in front of City Hall. At one point the judge sent his bailiff out into the street to demand to know what was going on, and why they were building the damned thing right in the street.

"Mr. Locke's instructions," Gavin James said, and the bailiff went back inside to deliver that message to the judge.

"All right, William," Judge Tinsley said. "That's all."

The bailiff exited the office, leaving Judge Tinsley with his closest associate, if not friend, Gordon Vestal.

"This is not working out quite the way we envisioned, Gordon," Tinsley said, shaking his head. "This man Locke is entirely too efficient."

"Give it time, Judge," Vestal said. "A man who relies on a bottle can't function without it forever. I've been keeping an eye on him and he's already had too much to drink once. It should happen again."

"What if he doesn't?" the judge asked. "What if he no longer has the filthy habit?"

"How many drunks do you know who can stay away from whiskey or beer, Judge?" Vestal asked. "Don't worry, he'll slip up."

"Well, it better be soon," Tinsley said, "or we're having a hanging this Saturday."

"Don't worry, Ansel," Vestal said, "all will go according to plan."

"What about that idiot partner of yours?"

"He doesn't know a thing," Vestal said, "nor does he suspect anything."

"At least that is going according to plan," the other man said.

"You've got to calm down, Ansel. Just leave it all to me. I'll handle everything."

"You'd better!" Judge Tinsley said. "You're the one who got me involved in this in the first place."

"And I'm the one who is going to put a lot of money into your pockets," Vestal shot back, "don't forget that!"

"All right, all right," the judge said, "there's no point in fighting each other. You're right, I should remain calm—"

"That's right."

"—at least until there is something to get excited about."

THIRTY

Walking around town Locke spotted the fliers nailed up on every available surface. Now and then he'd encounter a cluster of people standing around one, reading the announcement, talking excitedly. And it soon became evident to him that the town folks recognized him on sight. Suddenly, the air in Fredericksburg was alive with anticipation. He could feel it.

The three men riding into town were dressed in worn clothes, over which they wore serapes. They had cartridge belts crisscrossed over their chests, and sombreros on their heads. Mustaches and several days' growth of beard adorned their faces, making them look dirty and dangerous. Their appearance screamed out bandidos, and people in the street avoided them.

One was called Enrique, a dour faced man who always looked as if he had lost his last peso. Another was Luis, who if he did not look as perpetually worried as Enrique, looked doubtful. Perhaps they were anxious about the task that had been assigned to them. A great deal of money was at stake. All they had to do was live long enough to collect it.

The third was the youngest, barely twenty, and here for all the world to see was the ready smile of a happy young man. He enjoyed being a bandido and hoped one day to lead his own band. His name was Wilfredo.

The three bandidos dismounted in front of the saloon that declared it had "Whiskey and Gambling" inside. They were going to need whiskey to do what they had to do.

As they entered the saloon all eyes went to them. With a bandido in the jail at the moment, many of the men wondered what the hell these three were thinking coming to town like this, but no one was willing to ask them about it.

When they reached the bar Enrique said, "Whiskey," to Ben Ames.

"Comin' up," the barkeep answered. To him their money was as good as anyone else's, and if they tried anything, he had his shotgun behind the bar. It was a side-by-side Greener and he was quite willing to give them both barrels if they did something to deserve or demand it.

He set them all up with shots of red-eye and withdrew but not quite far enough to be totally out of earshot.

"I do not like this," Luis said.

"What is it you do not like, compadre?" Enrique asked. "The whiskey?"

"You know what I mean," Luis said. "This is a dangerous man."

"He was a dangerous man," Enrique said. "Now he is an old dog with no teeth."

Although Wilfredo was the youngest, all three men were in their twenties. It was Enrique, though, who spoke with the arrogance of youth. Belying his worrisome countenance, Enrique had the confidence that he and Luis and Wilfredo would be able to perform their task successfully.

Luis downed his drink and said, "I need another."

"No," Enrique said, "you do not. One is for courage, two is a celebration, and we have nothing to celebrate yet. We will come back . . . after."

"You are confident we can do this?" Luis asked.

"I am," Wilfredo said, but the other two ignored him. They both thought he was an idiot.

"Would I have volunteered if I was not confident?" Enrique asked. "Look at it this way, amigo. Once this man was famous, feared, he was El Viudador. Now he is old and slow. But when we kill him, we will be the men who killed *El Viudador*, the Widowmaker." Enrique slapped his partner on the back heartily. "It is we who will be famous and feared then, eh?"

"Famous and feared," Luis said, shaking his head. "I will be satisfied with alive."

THIRTY-ONE

Gordon Vestal looked out the window of his bedroom, just above the store he and Ed Hansen owned. Hansen lived in a house several blocks away. Vestal, as the senior partner, had taken these rooms upstairs.

"What are you looking at?" the woman asked from his bed.

"Just the street," he said.

"You're neglecting me to look at a dusty street?"

There was a pout in her tone, but it did not ring true. He turned and looked at her. She was lovely, naked beneath the thin sheet so that he could see the contours of her body beneath it clearly. Her breasts were full, but firm, and her nipples were hard, making small nubs in the sheet. Her bare shoulders were pale and smooth, and her dark hair cascaded down around them. She was an enthusiastic lover, but Vestal never lost sight of the fact that they were the same—opportunistic and ambitious. Fredericksburg was just a stop for both of them.

"I'm not neglecting you at all, my love," he said. "If I come over to that bed right now you'll miss your appointment with Mr. Locke."

She sat up in bed, holding the sheet so that it would not fall away from her.

"You have a point," she said, "and he is rather dashing, don't you think?"

He turned to look at her, quite comfortable with his own nudity. "My love, I believe that in Mr. Locke you have finally found a man who is immune to your charms."

She allowed the sheet to fall away, revealing her perfect breasts, and said, "Don't be so sure of that, Gordon."

He felt a stirring in his loins at the sight of her and said, "I believe you are going to be late for Mr. Locke, Nina. . . ."

"When did you realize you were good with a gun?" Nina asked.

They were walking to a small restaurant off of Front Street that Nina said she thought Locke would like. She suggested that they wouldn't be stared at as they had been in The Dexter House. She had been a few minutes late, but Locke didn't care.

"Is this an interview question?"

"No, not yet. We can wait until we're seated."

When they entered the restaurant they were watched by fewer people only because the place was smaller than The Dexter.

"Didn't make much difference, did it?" she asked as they were seated.

"They'll get bored and go back to their dinner."

"You're pretty confident about your ability to read people, aren't you?"

"Now, is this part of the interview?"

"No," she said, again, "not yet."

When she finally did ask a prepared question during dinner he had to ask again if it was for the interview. She finally said, "Yes."

He sat back and looked at her, pushing away his plate. He picked up his coffee cup while he considered the question.

"When did I realize I was good with a gun?" She'd started with that same question.

"Is that a difficult question?"

"Only because as far back as I can remember I could use a gun. To pinpoint when I knew I could is difficult." It also seemed to be a silly question to him. He'd never agreed to an interview before because he thought the questions would be silly. So far he was right.

Nina pushed her plate away to clear a space on the table in front of her to make notes. She wrote something down, apparently based on what he'd just said, and then started asking more questions about his past. After about half an hour she stopped and set aside her pencil and paper. From his side of the table Locke could see she'd written one sentence.

"Is there a problem?"

"You're not telling me anything about yourself."

He remained silent.

"You're not going to tell me anything about yourself, are you?"

"Miss Ballinger—"

"Nina," she said, "please . . . at least for tonight."

"Nina . . . I'm doing the best I can."

"We had a deal," she said, "and I kept my part of it. Now it's time for you to keep your word."

"I'm trying."

"Honestly?"

He nodded.

"This is the best you can do?"

"With the questions you're asking, yes."

She sat back in her chair and glared at him.

"I have done hundreds of interviews."

"I'm sure you have."

"And no one has ever complained before."

"I wasn't complaining."

"I suppose you think you could do better?" she asked. "If you were interviewing you?"

"No," he said, "I'm not—"

"Go ahead," she invited, folding her arms across her chest. She had dressed for dinner, and this was the first time he was seeing her in an actual dress. It had a high neck, but was tucked at the waist and showed off her full figure. If he was a man looking for a woman, he wouldn't have to look any further.

"You want me to interview myself?"

"Why not?"

Locke looked around the room, located the waiter, and called him over.

"You won't do it?" she asked.

"No."

"Why not?"

"Because it's ridiculous. This interview was your idea."

"And you gave your word—"

"If you ask the right questions," Locke said, cutting her off, "you'll get the right answers."

"All right, then," Nina said. "Let's go to my office where we can sit in a more businesslike atmosphere and I'll ask the right questions."

"Fine," Locke said. Unencumbered by the need to pay a check they both headed for the door, once again tracked by every eye in the house.

Enrique and Luis saw Locke walking down the street earlier with a woman and watched as they went into a restaurant. Wilfredo was looking at two young girls who were walking by—and, naturally, was smiling. Enrique slapped his chest to get his attention.

"You see?" Enrique said. "We did not even have to go and find him. This is meant to be."

"What do we do now?" Luis asked. "Go in after him?"

"No," Enrique said, "we will wait for him outside and take him in the street, for all to see. Once he is out of the way getting Ignacio out will be—how do the gringos say?—a piece of pie?"

It was dusk when Locke and Nina left the restaurant. It would probably be dark in fifteen more minutes. Locke was angry because he thought Nina was playing word games, but he also had the feeling that if he talked to her—really talked to her, and said everything out loud—that he might solve some of his own problems. Maybe it was time to talk to someone about Tombstone—but a newspaperwoman?

"Look—" he said. He was starting to turn toward her when something caught his eye and his instincts kicked in immediately.

"Down!" he shouted. He grabbed her and pulled her to the ground just as the first volley of shots came from across the street, shattering the front window of the restaurant.

THIRTY-TWO

Locke kept his body on top of Nina's as the broken glass rained down on them. The shots kept coming so he grabbed her and dragged her behind a horse trough.

"What's going on?" she shouted.

"Are you all right?"

"I think so," she said, checking herself for wounds, "but what—"

"Just stay down!" he said, drawing his gun. "This may be Colon's gang trying to break him out."

"Great!" she said. "And I'm here to see it! This'll be great for the paper."

He stared at her a moment and then said, "Let's hope you live to write it and I live to read it."

"Locke—"

"Just stay down, Nina," he warned, putting his hand on her head and pushing, "and don't come up until I come for you, or help comes."

"Oh, yeah, help," she shouted after him, "from whom?"

The firing had stopped. Locke was lying at one end of the horse trough while Nina was at the other. The street was quiet as people had taken cover. The only sound was water running out a hole that a bullet had punched into the side of the trough.

Locke had to risk taking a look. He needed to know how many there were and where they were. From the number of shots fired he was figuring three, maybe four. As to who they were there were two possibilities. Someone had either recognized him and was trying to make a name for himself, or Ignacio Colon's men were trying to kill him. Either way, it was necessary to locate the shooters.

He got to his knees and peered over the top of the horse trough. Whoever had fired at him had taken cover, or was gone. Off to his right was a buckboard that someone had abandoned when taking cover. He took a deep breath, sprang to his feet, and ran for it. The firing started again. He fired as he ran, at the same time locating the source of the shots. He counted three points of origin as he launched himself into a dive that took him onto the buckboard. Once he landed, the firing stopped again, but he'd found out what he wanted. Two men were firing from two different doorways, and one had taken cover behind some barrels.

He looked around him to make sure he was alone in the buckboard. He had fired two covering shots, so he quickly ejected those shells and inserted two live ones. He had six shots, and there were three assailants, probably armed with rifles and pistols, from the sounds the shots had made. What he needed was another gun, or some help, and it didn't sound like any was coming.

Knowing what he knew about Sheriff Horrigan, he didn't imagine the man was hurrying to his aid.

He went over his options. He could wait for them to make the first move, or he could force the issue. If they had checked out the town then they should have known they had little to fear from the law. That meant they could afford to be patient, if they really wanted to get him this time, and not have to leave it for another. On the other hand somebody other than the law might decide to help him, and they wouldn't want that. They'd want to get to him while he was still alone. That meant they were likely to make the first move.

He decided to sit and wait. He took off his hat and chanced using one eye to watch the street.

Enrique was angry. That hijo de un cabrón, Wilfredo, had rushed his first shot, stepping out into the open to take it. He had not only missed, but had alerted Locke to their presence, and the man had taken cover. When the gringo ran from the horse trough to the buckboard Enrique knew he had done it to draw fire and locate them. But even he had not been able to resist the urge and had fired one shot, giving himself away.

Now El Viudador knew where they were, but it was still tres against uno. He could remain in the back of that buckboard all day if he wanted to. They had to make the first move. If all three of them rushed the buckboard, at least one of them would get him.

"Luis?"

"Sí?" Luis was in the next doorway. Wilfredo had taken

cover behind some barrels that had been stacked in front of a store.

"If we rush him we can take him?"

"He will get one of us," Luis reasoned, "perhaps even two."

"But one of us will get him!"

There was no answer.

"Perhaps he will only get one—Wilfredo."

He looked over to where Wilfredo was crouched. The younger man did not seem to be able to hear their conversation.

"We will let him go first, and we will run behind him."

Still no answer.

"It will work!" Enrique said.

Silence, and then, "Perhaps."

"You are closer to Wilfredo," Enrique said. "You tell him the plan. Tell him we will count to three then charge the buckboard. He is an idiot. He will do it. We will let him go on three and we will go on four."

Luis thought it over, and then said, "All right. I will tell him."

"Bueno!"

"We will go on four?" Luis asked, double-checking.

"Sí."

"All right, I will tell him."

Of course, Enrique had every intention of going on five, but Luis did not need to know that.

THIRTY-THREE

There was no way for Locke to get his hands on another gun, so he was going to have to make every shot count. As he watched, the two men in the doorways seemed to be having a conversation, but he didn't want to risk a shot from this distance. With a rifle he might have, but if he took a shot and missed and they charged, he'd be down to five rounds.

Jesus, there was a time he never would have even thought about the possibility of missing.

He really needed a drink.

There were three, Locke figured, and one of them had to be the leader. If they charged him, they'd send the most disposable man first. That's what he would have done. And the leader would go last, figuring he'd have the best shot at getting Locke, and surviving.

Locke watched and waited. If they came for him one behind the other then his figuring was right. But if they came three abreast they might get him, because he wouldn't know which one to take first.

Sure could use another gun.

*   *   *

"Is he ready?" Enrique asked.

"Sí, he is ready," Luis said.

Idiots, Enrique thought, both of them.

"Luis, you count."

"Uno," Luis said, loudly, "dos . . . tres!"

Wilfredo stood up, shouted something, and ran toward the buckboard, firing his gun.

Cuatro, Enrique thought, and watched Luis leave the cover of his doorway, and then, Cinco!

Single file! They were coming for him single file, as he'd hoped.

As the second man broke from his doorway Locke jumped to his feet, but he did not fire, yet. Instead, he jumped onto the buckboard seat, giving himself an even higher vantage point. Bullets whizzed around him as the first man fired wildly. As the second man prepared to fire, the third man broke from his cover. Locke, feeling remarkably calm and steady, fired once at the third man. The bullet took him in the chest and brought a shocked look to his face just before he fell.

The second man fired twice, and one shot hit Locke in the hip. He stood fast, though, and fired at the first man, who was now getting too close to miss no matter how wildly he let fly. Locke's bullet hit him in the belly, driving him back a few feet before he crumpled to the ground.

Locke had four shots left and turned his attention to the second man.

If Luis had fired without thinking he might have killed

Locke and gotten out of town alive. But he was shocked when Wilfredo went down in front of him and when he turned and saw that Enrique had gone down behind him. By the time he turned his attention back to John Locke it was too late. Locke fired a third time, and it was all over.

"That was amazing!" Nina Ballinger proclaimed, moments later. She hurried to the buckboard and looked up at Locke, who was hurriedly reloading, just in case.

"You just stood up there and shot it out with them, and you got all three!"

Reloaded, he stepped down from the buckboard, but when his right foot hit the ground the leg gave beneath him and he fell.

"Locke!" Nina Ballinger rushed to his side and grabbed his arm. "You're hurt."

He looked up at her and said, "You didn't think there could be that much lead flying around without me getting hit by a slug, did you?"

He used her and the buckboard to get back to his feet. When he looked he saw that his entire right pant leg was soaked with blood.

"You need a doctor," she said.

"First I've got to check the three of them and make sure they're dead."

Others had gathered around the bodies, as the townspeople returned to the street to talk about what they just saw. Some of them were looking at Locke in as much awe as Nina Ballinger.

John Locke started walking toward the bodies when someone called out, "Stop right there, Locke!"

He turned his head and saw Sheriff Horrigan standing in the street, facing him. The foolish man still had his gun holstered.

"You're too late, Sheriff," Locke said. "The action is over."

"I told you I didn't want any shootouts in my town," the lawman said.

"Well, I guess you forgot to tell them." Locke was still eyeing the three downed men. He wasn't sure one of them wouldn't have a last ditch effort in him before he expired. When involved in any kind of firefight he always checked afterward to make sure the men were dead before he holstered his gun.

He started toward the men.

"I said stand fast!" Horrigan shouted.

"Sheriff, you're shouting at the wrong man," Nina Ballinger said. "Those three men bushwacked Mr. Locke and almost killed us both."

"This is none of your affair, Miss Ballinger."

"I beg to differ, sir," she said. "I was right in the middle of the whole thing."

While Nina engaged the sheriff in conversation, Locke limped over to the men and checked them in turn. Even when he was satisfied that they were dead he kicked their guns away from them. Then and only then did he holster his weapon and turn back to the sheriff.

"Where were you when the shooting was going on?" Nina demanded.

"I—I was at the other end of town," he said. "I got here as fast as I could."

"I rather doubt that, Sheriff."

Horrigan decided not to waste any more time on the newspaper editor.

"Locke, I'll have your gun."

"Sheriff," John Locke said, "after what just happened if you want my gun you're going to have to come and take it."

"I'll do it if I have to," the lawman said, flexing the fingers of his gunhand as it hung down by his holster.

Locke got closer and said lower, so the gathering townspeople could not hear him.

"Frankly, Sheriff," he said, "I don't think you're man enough to do it, but you're welcome to try."

Horrigan stared at Locke for a few moments. He wanted to try, but he was affected by the obvious lack of respect Locke showed.

Suddenly, he turned and addressed the crowd.

"All right, I need some volunteers to take these men to the undertaker's."

As the lawman moved away Nina Ballinger once again took Locke's arm and said, "Let's get you to the doctor's."

THIRTY-FOUR

Doc Stone pressed on Locke's hip, causing him to catch his breath.

"Damn it, Doc!" Locke snapped.

"Looks and feels worse than it is, Mr. Locke," Stone said. "Bullet took a chunk out of your thigh, but there's no lead in you."

"That's good news," Locke said. "Didn't even feel it until I put my full weight on that leg."

"Shock," Stone said. "From what I heard there was a lot going on around you to keep you busy. I'll finish cleaning it up and then bandage it, and you should be good as new in a few weeks."

"Few weeks?"

"You should stay off this leg—"

"Can't do that, Doc," Locke said. "I got a hanging to officiate."

Stone stopped what he was doing and straightened so he could look Locke in the eye. To this point he'd been talking to the man's thigh.

"If you don't stay off that leg I can't guarantee the bleeding won't start again. You've got to give this wound time to heal, man."

"After Ignacio Colon swings on Saturday, Doc, I'll have all the time in the world. Just bandage it up good and tight, will you?"

"I'll do the best I can," Stone said. "I hope this town is paying you enough for this."

"They are."

"You'll need a new pair of trousers, anyway. These are stained with blood and I had to cut 'em up pretty good."

"That's okay, Doc," Locke said, "I know just where to get a pair."

Locke limped into Gordon Vestal's store just ahead of the man. He'd gone to Vestal's house and taken the man away from dinner in order to open the store and get him some new pants.

"Well, take your pick," Vestal said. "In fact, take more than one pair, and then I'll get back to my dinner."

"I guess the shooting didn't attract your attention, huh?" Locke asked.

"The shooting took place at the other end of town, remember? I didn't hear a thing."

Locke started to reach up to a shelf but the motion caused some pull on his bandages.

"Would you get me those, please?"

"These?" Vestal stepped past him and took down a pair of jeans. Locke checked the size and nodded.

"I'll take two, as you suggested."

"Fine." Vestal got him another pair. "Is that all?"

"I need another gun," Locke said.

"There's a gunsmith's shop in town," Vestal said. "I have

some rifles, ammunition, but you'll find a better selection over there."

Since it was late, Locke took the suggestion. He could check in with the gun shop in the morning and get a handgun free of charge. He just needed a second one to back up the first, in case something like today's incident happened again.

As Vestal was locking the door behind them he said, "From what I heard it sounds like you acquitted yourself quite well today."

"Did you expect less?"

"No, no," Vestal said, straightening. "It just seems like we hired the right man for the job."

That had been said to him several times already, between Vestal and the judge. Never before, however, had it sounded quite so insincere.

THIRTY-FIVE

Locke limped back to his hotel and found Nina Ballinger waiting for him in the lobby.

"I lost you after we took you to the doctor," she said. "Are you all right?"

"Fine," Locke said. "The bullet just took a piece of me and kept going."

"I still can't believe what I saw today," she said, wide-eyed. "You just stood straight up and shot it out with them, and with all those bullets flying through the air you were only wounded once?"

"I didn't just stand up," Locke argued. "I had a plan."

"I'd like to hear about it."

"Nina—"

"No, no," she said, waving her hands impatiently. "You've been putting me off with this interview you agreed to—no matter what you say about me asking the wrong questions. But this . . . you killed three men today, before they could kill you. That's news and I have to cover it. Now, I could write it the way I saw it—which you seem to feel is wrong—or I could listen to your side and write that. It's your choice."

Locke studied her for a moment, was about to put her off yet again, then thought better of it. Maybe he could put her and her newspaper to good use.

"All right."

"What?" She seemed surprised.

"I said, okay. Let's go into the saloon and we'll talk about it."

"Well . . . well, all right!" she said, excitedly. "Let's go."

They walked into the hotel bar.

"I'll get you a beer," Nina said. "You go and sit down and rest your leg."

The place was quiet, since it offered no girls and no gambling. All it sold was drinks, mostly to its guests. Locke took a table in the rear, placed his back firmly against the wall, and waited for Nina to return with two beers.

"All right," she said, sitting opposite him and taking out a notebook and a pencil. "Let me tell you what I saw and then you can tell me what I missed, what only you know. . . ."

They talked for half an hour and when they were done Nina had filled many pages of her small notebook. Locke's beer was gone, but Nina's had only a few sips missing.

"Oh," she said, looking up from her writing and spotting his empty mug, "do you want another?"

"No," he said, firmly.

Locke was surprised at his own resolve. Of course, he hadn't yet had time to be alone since the shooting, going from the doctor to Vestal's store and then back here with Nina. He hadn't had much time to even think about what happened, which was another reason he had agreed to talk to Nina Ballinger. While explaining everything to her he was able to examine it himself.

He had been rock steady from the time the first shot was fired until the last. It had been a while since he'd been involved in a firefight like that. In his youth he'd traded lead with the best of them, even in Tombstone, which was not that long ago. Since Tombstone, however, and since returning from his drunken year in Mexico the jobs he'd taken had been simple ones. Mostly as a guide or a tracker. In fact, he thought today was the first day he'd killed a man in almost three years.

Maybe he wasn't as far gone as he thought.

"Well," Nina said, moments later, "I think I've got all I need."

"You're going to write that tonight?"

"Right away," she said, pushing her chair back. "I'll have Augustus set it first thing in the morning. It'll be out in our afternoon edition, front page."

"Don't bill this as an interview," he warned.

"I'm going to headline it as an eyewitness account," she said. "Then I'll write what you explained to me. So, you weren't ever afraid?"

Not during, he thought.

"There was no time," he said. "I had you to think of, an innocent bystander—do you know if anyone in the restaurant was hurt?"

"We're here to decide whether or not John Locke should continue to hold the position as marshal of Tombstone. In light of the fact that he's killed some ten men

since he took office—one of them by accident—because he'd been drinking—"

"I went back and checked," she said. "They lost their window, but that was about it. No customers were injured, at least not by gunfire. Just some cuts and bruises."

He nodded.

"And the sheriff sure was no help," she said. "You can believe I'm going to write that he was nowhere in sight."

"Good," he said. "Also write this. Say that I'm not all that sure what's going on in this town, but the one thing I am sure of is that Ignacio Colon is going to hang on Saturday. That's what I'm being paid to do, and it's going to happen."

She scribbled hurriedly into her notebook and then said, "Got it. Will you be up and around tomorrow?"

Locke stretched his leg. His wound was throbbing, and his leg felt stiff.

"I'll be up," he said. "There are things that need to be done."

"All right, then," she said. "I'll see you tomorrow. You can finish my beer, if you like."

Locke looked at the mug, then said, "No thanks."

She tucked her notebook and pencil away, then stood there and looked at him for a moment.

"What?" he asked.

"You saved my life today," she said. "Don't think I'll forget that."

"It was a reflex—"

"Yes, I know," she said. "It was all reflex, but I thank you, anyway."

Impulsively, she moved to his side of the table and planted a kiss on his cheek.

"Thank you, for everything."

" 'Snothing," he muttered, embarrassed.

She smiled, then laughed at how uncomfortable the kiss made him, and left the hotel.

Locke eyed her unfinished, almost untouched beer for a few more moments before hauling himself to his feet and painfully climbing the stairs to the second floor. Tomorrow he'd ask for a first floor room.

THIRTY-SIX

Locke remained in his room the rest of the evening, took some pills the doctor had given him for the pain, and fell asleep until he was awakened by the early light streaming through the window.

When he returned to his room the night before he had settled down on the bed to wait for the shakes to come, and the need for a drink—but they never did. This surprised him. While he was not a full-fledged drunk—anymore—he was still susceptible to the need for it. Occasionally—like the other night—the urge came unbidden, but it always came—at least, over the past few years—after an incident like today's. He thought back over the day's events, and he marveled—as had Nina Ballinger—at how efficiently and coldly he had reacted during the gunfight. Apparently, his own opinions of his diminishing skill and nerve were wrong. There was still more to John Locke than met the eye— even his own eye.

Rising and dressing were chores, but he managed it without bringing forth any new leakage from his wound. Some blood had seeped through the bandages, but they were certainly not soaked in it. The doctor had done an excellent job of binding him.

He left his room and went down to the lobby to inquire about another room, this time on the first floor.

"Of course, sir," the clerk said. "We have our instructions to give you anything you need. I can give you room five, at the end of our downstairs hall."

"That's fine."

"Would you like me to have your belongings moved there? I mean, since the stairs present a problem for you in your present condition?"

"That would be good," Locke said. "Thanks."

"No problem, sir. I'll have it done immediately."

Locke nodded and went outside. He could hear hammering coming from the vicinity of the City Hall and walked in that direction. When he came in view of the construction he saw Gavin James and his helpers had made remarkable progress. The structure even looked like it was going to be a gallows. He wondered if Ignacio Colon could see it from his cell window. He decided to go over to the jail and find out. He wanted to talk with the sheriff, anyway.

Sheriff Horrigan scowled when Locke entered his office.

"I suppose you're here to further berate me," Horrigan said.

"You don't even talk like a sheriff, Horrigan," Locke said. "What did you do before you took this job?"

"I was a . . . a schoolteacher."

"From teacher to lawman? Not a very logical jump."

"I was born in the East. And you don't talk much like a gunfighter."

"What a coincidence. I was born in the East, as well."

"Really? Where?"

"That's not what I'm here to talk about."

"Well . . . what are you here to talk about?"

"The three men I killed yesterday," Locke said. "Have you identified them?"

"Nobody knows their names," Horrigan said, "but I have several men who say they think at least two of them ride—or rode—with Colon and his bandidos. They were obviously here to break him out."

"No," Locke said, "they were here to kill me. The break would have come later."

"So what do you think will happen next?" the lawman asked. "The break, or another attempt on your life?"

"I don't know," Locke said. "The three of them may have been sent to town to test me."

"For what?"

"To see how good I was." Or how good he still was, but he didn't voice that thought.

"Well, I guess they found out."

"I'd like to see Colon," Locke said. "Maybe he can tell us who they were."

"I'm not taking him over to the undertaker's to identify the bodies," Horrigan said. "I'm not letting him out until he hangs."

"That suits me."

Horrigan nodded, got his keys, and let Locke into the cell block.

"What happened?" Carlos Mendoza asked the gringo.

Hernando Juarez stood behind the gringo and slightly to his left. The others fanned out around him because they also wanted to hear the news. The gringo looked nervous, and licked his lips before speaking.

"He killed them."

"All three?" Mendoza asked.

"All three."

The others began to murmur. Mendoza silenced them with a chopping motion of his hand.

"Tell me what happened?"

The gringo recounted the shootout to Mendoza, eliciting more murmuring from the others, who nevertheless remained silent until he was done with his story.

"Is that the truth?" Hernando Juarez asked.

"Yes."

"Did you see this?"

"I didn't," the man said, "but there were many witnesses."

Juarez looked at Mendoza.

"It seems El Viudador is still very formidable, Carlos."

"Perhaps," Mendoza said, "or perhaps we simply sent the wrong men."

"Or not enough," Juarez said.

Mendoza waved a hand, clearly annoyed.

He looked at the gringo. "What about the sheriff? His deputies?"

"Useless."

"You said John Locke was wounded?"

The man nodded. "I don't know how badly, though."

"Go back and find out," Mendoza said. "The hanging is tomorrow. We must make a move by then, and I want all the information we can get. By tomorrow we will have Ignacio back, and this will all be over."

"W-what will you do when you have him back?"

"If I know Ignacio," Mendoza said, "he will have us burn the town to the ground."

"B-but . . . that wasn't part of the agreement."

"Ah yes, the agreement . . ."

THIRTY-SEVEN

Ignacio Colon watched as John Locke approached his cell. The bandido sat up on his cot, his feet on the floor.

"Are you going to visit me every day?" he asked.

"What's the difference?" Locke asked. "Tomorrow's your last day on earth."

"Ah, yes," Colon said. "I can see your gallows from my window. I am flattered to have all that work done for me."

"You won't be so flattered tomorrow."

"Perhaps."

"I don't suppose you heard about the shooting in the street yesterday?"

Colon shrugged. "Who would tell me? And no one gives me a newspaper in here. You're limping, so I guess you were involved."

"Three of your men tried to bushwack me when I was coming out of a restaurant with a lady."

"A lady?"

"Miss Ballinger."

"Oh, yes, the newspaper editor," Colon said. "The one who called for my head. Tell me, was she harmed?"

"No," Locke said, "and your men didn't make it."

"How many did you kill?"

"All that were sent against me," Locke said. "Three."

"El Viudador still has the talent for killing, I see," Colon commented.

"A talent for self-preservation, is more like it."

"In any case," Colon said, "they were just testing you."

"I figured that," Locke said. "If they had the time they'd send more men, try again. But there is only one more day."

"Then perhaps they will come today," Colon said. "Today for you, and then tomorrow for me. It would be easier to rescue me tomorrow without you around to . . . officiate."

"I had thought of that," Locke said. "Maybe I'll just stay in here with you, where it's safe."

"I do not think you will do that."

"Why not?"

"The food is horrible," Colon said, "and there are no women."

"Small prices to pay for staying alive, I'd say."

Colon stood up and studied Locke through the bars, then shook his head.

"No, you are not the kind of man to hide. Not El Viudador." Then Colon's eyes went to the gun in Locke's holster, studying the specially crafted grip. "But the stories I have heard, they say that El Viudador may not be the man, but the gun—that gun."

Locke looked down and then removed the gun from his holster.

"This gun?" Locke's fingers fit comfortably in the grooved handle of the weapon.

Colon looked into Locke's eyes, and then at the gun.

"I could kill you now and save the town the trouble of hanging you."

"And waste that beautiful gallows you are having built in my honor?" Colon asked. "I think not. Besides, that is not what you were paid to do."

"I don't know," Locke said, "it might be worth the money I'd lose."

Colon ignored the comment and concentrated on the gun, again. "That is a Peacemaker, is it not?"

"Basic 1873 Peacemaker design," Locke said, "with a few modifications." The contoured grip and cutdown barrel were the basic modifications. Like Bat Masterson, Locke liked a shorter barrel on his gun, so he had the normal 7½ inch barrel cut down to 5. Masterson, ever the perfectionist, had his cut down to 4½ inches.

"Peacemaker," Colon said, "Widowmaker. That is very catchy. Tell me, does the name refer to you or the gun?"

Locke examined the weapon in his hand, and then holstered it.

"Guess you'll never know."

"Not even as a dying request?"

"I'm going to describe to you the three men I killed," Locke said. "Let's see if you can put a name to any of them."

Quickly, he rattled off what he had seen of the men, both when they were standing, and when they were on the ground.

"From what you say, how they looked, and the way they charged you, I'd say the young idiota who led the way was Wilfredo. The other two were most likely Luis and Enrique. Enrique, he would be the brains, if they had a brain among them."

"No last names?"

Colon shrugged.

"Who cares about last names? They would have been killed sooner or later."

"Who's going to lead the men in here to free you tomorrow, Ignacio?"

"Ah," Colon said, with his golden smile, "we are on a first name basis. Bueno, Juan. I told you before, Carlos Mendoza will lead them."

"And how many men do you have?"

"I had fourteen or fifteen," Colon said, "the last time I counted—but you have killed three."

"Why are you answering my questions?"

"I am nothing if not polite," Colon said. "Besides, Mendoza will recruit more men. There is no telling how many will come."

Colon walked to the bars and took hold of two of them, pressing his face between them.

"Perhaps you are right," he said, "this place just might be the safest for you."

"No, I think you were right," Locke said, turning to leave. He banged on the door.

"About what?" Colon asked.

"About me not being the type to hide."

The sheriff opened the door, allowing Locke to leave the block.

"And perhaps," Colon said, "that is just what I am counting on."

THIRTY-EIGHT

When Locke left the jailhouse he walked back to the City Hall, once again bringing him to the partially erected gallows. Gavin James saw him coming and paused in his work. He and the two other men were shirtless, with bandanas around their necks. All three were drenched with sweat.

"What do you think?" James asked as Locke approached the carpenter.

All the posts had been driven firmly into the ground, and the platform was almost complete. A stairway was still to be added. Across the way the viewing stand was almost done, as well.

"It looks like a gallows to me," Locke said. He turned and glanced over at the jail. He saw the window to Ignacio Colon's cell.

"Can he see it from there?" James asked.

"He can see it, all right."

"How is he?"

"Very calm."

"He must have nerves of steel," James said. "I'd go crazy watching my own gallows being built."

"It's easy to be calm when you believe you're not going to hang."

"He believes that?"

"Oh, yes, he's confident that his boys are going to come and save him in the nick of time."

"Why in the nick of time?" James asked. "Why not just break him out before tomorrow?"

"That's possible, too," Locke said, "but don't you think it would be easier for them to snatch him off this gallows than to break him out of a jail cell?"

James looked up at the fruits of his labor.

"Off my gallows?"

Locke nodded.

"I guess so. It is out in the open—but the street will be packed with people."

"And that could also work to their advantage," Locke pointed out.

"You're not painting a very successful picture for us," James said. "Do you expect to hang him or not?"

"Oh, I expect to hang him," Locke said, confidently, "I just don't expect it to be easy."

Before parting company with the carpenter Locke asked Gavin James when the gallows would be ready.

"We can test it tomorrow," he said. "Will your hangman be here by then?"

"He better be," Locke said.

James looked up at the gallows and said, "It's going even faster than I thought it would." He put his hand out to touch a post, almost lovingly.

"Well, anyway, I'll let you and your men get back to work."

James nodded, turned, and walked back to the other side of the scaffolding.

Locke went back to his hotel. As he entered the lobby he was waved over by the desk clerk.

"Your new key," the man said, handing it to him.

"Thanks."

"And Miss Ballinger dropped something off for you," he added. "I put it in your room . . . if that's all right?"

"Sure. Thanks, again."

"Just let us know what you need, sir."

"I will," Locke said, and then, "Oh, your other key." He turned over the old key, then walked down the hall to his new room.

As he entered he saw a stack of newspapers on the bed. He went over and looked at the top one. The front page read: WIDOWMAKER IN SHOOTOUT ON FREDERICKSBURG STREET. Underneath was added: JOHN LOCKE CALMLY KILLS THREE IN GUN BATTLE.

He counted the newspapers and saw that she had left him a dozen. What did she think he was going to do with them, put them in a scrapbook?

He picked all of them up and left the room.

THIRTY-NINE

When he reached the office of the *Fredericksburg Front Page* he was angrier than he had been when he left his hotel. Why he was angry to the degree he was he would worry about later. For now, he had some things to say.

When he entered it was quiet, Augustus was nowhere to be seen. The door to the office was wide open and Nina Ballinger saw him enter. As he approached her she smiled.

"I see you got the copies—"

He marched past her, slapped the twelve copies of the paper down on her desk, and then turned to glare at her.

"What did you think I needed so many copies for?" he demanded.

Taken aback by his anger she hesitated a moment, eyes wide, and then said, "I thought you might like to—to—"

"To what? Put them in a scrapbook? Do you think I have been cutting out articles all these years that describe how I killed some poor sap who was foolish enough to draw on me?"

"I—I didn't—"

"For Godsake, woman, I don't keep count!"

"I thought—I thought all gunfighters, er, kept—"

"I am not a gunfighter, Nina!"

"B-but—everything I've read—"

He still was not allowing her to mount any defense by finishing a sentence.

"What? What have you read?"

"Well . . ." She sidled past him to her desk, opened a drawer, and took out some yellowbacked books. He didn't even need to see them to know what they were. He knew the titles by heart. There was *The Widowmaker's Revenge*, and *Death and the Widowmaker*, and his favorite because it was so damned wrong, *The Smile on the Face of the Widowmaker*. This particular New York publisher had billed these books as part of its "Gunfighter series," lumping Locke in with killers like John Wesley Hardin and Buckskin Frank Leslie, or lawmen like Wyatt Earp and Bill Tilghman, or with real gunmen like Wild Bill Hickok and Ben Thompson. The only other book he'd ever really read any portion of was the one they did on Doc Holliday, and it was a pack of lies. For some reason, the one they published about Bat Masterson had been very complimentary—or so he'd been told.

He tossed the books onto the desk, on top of the newspapers.

"You know," he said, "at first you struck me as an intelligent woman."

She recoiled, as if he'd slapped her.

"I beg your pardon—"

"You should," he said, turning his back to leave, "you should . . ."

"Mr. Locke—"

He turned, still unwilling to let her complete a thought.

"Why would you believe something like that?" he demanded, pointing to the books on the desk. "Of all people, someone who is responsible for reporting news to the people accurately, why would you ever believe that—"

He stopped short, his anger overcoming his ability to form words, then turned and started out.

"Wait, wait!" she called. She ran after him and grabbed his arm.

He turned, pulling his arm away violently. She was holding his right arm, his gunhand and in that split second he was vulnerable.

"Don't!" he yelled.

She jumped back, more shocked by this reaction than by his anger.

"Good God!" she snapped. "What the hell is the matter with you?"

What was the matter with him was that he needed a drink. Suddenly, from out of nowhere, he needed a drink. His hands were shaking, and his mouth was dry. This was the reaction he had expected yesterday, after the shooting in the street. He was surprised to have it come on now.

"Are you all right?" Nina asked, suddenly solicitous.

"I—I'm fine," Locke said. He wanted to ask her if she had anything to drink in the place, but resisted. "Look, I'm sorry . . . I was raving . . . I don't like people to think they know me when they don't."

"I'm sorry, too," she said. "I didn't mean to offend you,

I just . . . you're right, I should know better than to believe what I read. It's just that . . . well, what you did yesterday, that . . . that is the stuff of myth."

"Not myth," he said. "If any of those men had been halfway decent with a gun I'd have been dead. I was just lucky they didn't send a better man after me."

"Well, what about today? They might send someone else."

"They could," he said, "but I think they'll just wait until tomorrow and come in for Colon."

"During the hanging?"

"That's my guess."

"How . . . how will you stop them?"

His insides were rattled. He kept his hands at his sides so she couldn't see his fingers quivering.

"I don't know," he said. "I honestly don't know."

FORTY

Locke stopped in the first saloon he saw, one he hadn't been in before. It was small and cramped, but had what he wanted. It was still early, so the place was empty. He ordered beer and then stared at it when the bartender placed it in front of him.

"Somethin' wrong with it?" the man asked.

"No," Locke said, "it's fine."

"Ain'tcha gonna drink it?"

Locke rubbed his palms on his thighs and licked his lips. He couldn't lose another night like he had before, not with the hanging coming up. He'd be dead for sure if he was anything but a hundred percent.

"No," he said, "no, I'm not."

"Well . . . ya still gotta pay." Apparently this barman had not heard about the council paying Locke's bills.

"That I'll do," Locke said, rather than argue. He tossed a coin up on the bar. "Thanks."

"For nothin'," the barman said, as Locke left.

Outside he took a deep breath and looked down at his hands. They were steady, but his guts were still knotted. Maybe some food and coffee would help.

He returned to the main street, intending to go to the café, but was brought up short by the man riding down the street toward him. He folded his arms across his chest and waited for the man to see him, and direct his horse over to him.

The man sat tall in his saddle. Locke knew that when his boot heels hit the ground he'd still be standing tall, nearly six foot six. Hanging from his saddle horn was a hangman's noose.

"You're standin' there like a man who owns this town," Arlo Hawkes said, looking down at Locke.

"Don't own it," Locke said, "just pretty much got the run of it."

Hawkes looked around, then said, "Bigger than I thought it'd be. Passed through here once a few years ago, weren't much then."

"They all grow, or die," Locke observed.

"This one is sure growin'," Hawkes said. "Where's a fella put his horse?"

"All the way at the end of the street," Locke said. "You'll pass your gallows on the way."

"Finished?"

"Pretty near."

"I'll need to test it."

"Tonight, or tomorrow."

"And how about a meal and a drink?"

"You'll pass a small café on your right," Locke said. "I'll be in there waiting for you. After we've eaten I'll take you over to the hotel. You won't have to pay for your room or food while you're here."

"That suits me," the hangman said. "See you in a few minutes."

He nudged his horse and continued down the street. As Locke watched him he realized the quivering in his stomach had stopped. Maybe having Arlo Hawkes in town calmed him. Of course, he knew the hangman's presence in town would have the opposite effect on most people. They'd be happy he was there, because that meant the hanging was going to go off as planned. But still, such a man made most people nervous.

After all, what kind of person made his living stretching necks?

FORTY-ONE

When Arlo Hawkes entered the café diners having lunch paused and stared. Although Hawkes was part Apache, it was his size that made him stand out. The floor vibrated beneath his feet when he walked, some of the boards groaning beneath his weight, yet as big and heavy as he was there was not an ounce of fat on his bones.

Locke had waited for Hawkes at the hotel instead of the café and gotten the man a room on the second floor. They put their greetings off until Hawkes had a chance to drop his gear in his room and have a bath. Even for a man who was only half Indian, Hawkes bathed more often than most men Locke had known. It was certainly not a bad habit, but it was disconcerting to a lot of people to have someone who looked like Hawkes almost always smelling like he'd just come from a bath. Locke thought it had something to do with the big man's success with women.

They agreed to meet later that afternoon for lunch, so by the time Hawkes arrived at the café he was famished.

"John," he said, joining Locke at a back table, "it's good to see you. It's been . . . what? About six months?"

Locke was a big man himself but his hand was engulfed in Hawkes's.

"About that," Locke agreed with a nod. "Thanks for coming on such short notice, Arlo."

Hawkes sat and for a moment everyone in the room waited to see if the wooden chair would hold him. When it did, they turned back to their meals. However, having Locke and Hawkes at the same table earned them furtive glances from time to time.

Locke picked up the coffeepot that was on the table and poured Hawkes a cup. If the hangman noticed the absence of anything alcoholic he did not mention it.

"I ordered us each a steak," Locke said. "They're not half bad here."

"That's okay," Hawkes said. "I'm not as fussy as you. I could eat a mule—and I have."

"It's that Indian blood," Locke said.

Hawkes smiled and said, "Serves me well in other ways, too."

The waiter came at that moment with the steaks. He nervously set them down in front of each man.

"When you come back," Hawkes said to him in a bass that sounded like it came from deep in his broad chest, "bring me a beer."

"Of course," the waiter said, then looked at Locke and asked, "Sir?"

"Not for me."

As the waiter moved away Hawkes picked up his knife and fork and began sawing into the meat.

"Still having one a day?" he asked, without looking directly at Locke.

"Mostly."

"I could never survive on that diet."

Locke knew that Hawkes's appetites in all areas were as prodigious as the man. Food, drink, and women in particular.

"Well," Hawkes said, "run it down for me. What are we facing?"

Quickly, Locke related the situation as the hangman plowed through his steak and vegetables, and went three mugs of beer. Locke continued to wash his own food down with coffee, ordering a second pot.

"So it's you and me against the world again?" Hawkes asked.

"There's a sheriff, and some deputies, but I don't think they'll be much help. Oh, and a bartender who volunteered his shotgun."

"Take him up on it," the big man said. "You mind if I have another steak?"

"Go ahead," Locke said. "We're not paying, the town is."

"In that case . . ." he said, and called over the waiter to order two more.

"Well, actually it ain't just you and me," Hawkes said, then.

"What do you mean?"

"Ran into a friend of yours, told him about this. He'll be here later today."

"A friend?"

"That's what he said."

"Who?"

"Ain't gonna tell you, yet."

"Why not?"

" 'cause if he don't show up, you'll hold it against him, and maybe me for gettin' your hopes up."

"If he can use a gun he's welcome."

"He can use one," Hawkes said. "Let's see if he shows up. He had some other business to attend to first."

The waiter came back with the second steak, and promised the third in a few minutes.

"Bring vegetables, too," Hawkes said. "More potatoes and carrots and whatever else you got."

"Yes, sir," the worried waiter said.

"He's afraid you're going to eat the kitchen empty," Locke said.

"There's got to be other restaurants in a town this size," Hawkes said.

"One or two decent ones," Locke said. "I'll take you to The Dexter House for dinner. It's where all the local bigwigs eat."

"The men we're workin' for?"

"Yep."

"Good," Hawkes said, around a huge chunk of meat in his mouth, "I want to meet them."

Locke smiled. "And I want them to meet you."

FORTY-TWO

Locke had a third pot of coffee while Hawkes polished off his third helping of steak with all the trimmings, washing it all down with six mugs of beer. By the time they were finished the other diners had gone as lunch time was over.

"Are you finally full?" Locke asked.

Hawkes burped, rubbed his stomach, and smiled. "When's dinner?"

"Later," Locke said. "First I'll take you to meet the men who are paying us."

"The men you don't trust?" Hawkes had listened carefully to everything Locke said while he was eating, even though he may not have looked as if he was.

"I just don't think they're telling us everything," Locke said.

"Telling you," Hawkes pointed out. "They haven't told me a thing, at all."

"Come on," Locke said, standing. "After you meet Vestal I'll take you to the judge and you can decide for yourself. And on the way I'll show you the gallows."

"Always like to see where I'm going to do my job," Hawkes said.

Although Hawkes kept his black hair cut shorter than the rest of his Indian ancestors he never covered it with a hat. The only thing about him that gave away his white heritage were his mother's blue eyes. He'd suffered some humiliation growing up Apache in a white world, raised mostly by his mother, but it had only taken one spurt of growth to stop it all when he turned thirteen. At fifteen he beat a man to death for putting his hands on his mother. He served two years in Yuma, and came out at seventeen having not only served in the prison but having conquered it, as well. Prisoners and guards alike were happy to see him go. That one stretch in jail had taught him a valuable lesson, and he never served another day since his release, fifteen years earlier. His mother had died of an illness while he was inside, but he never mentioned it—not then, and not now.

The two men stepped outside and scanned the street across the way. Hawkes had his Winchester in his hands, but had left his saddlebags and bedroll in his hotel room. Locke had his hand hovering down near his Peacemaker. He did not want to chance walking into another ambush. The first had almost killed him and Nina Ballinger.

"Damn heat," Locke said. He could already feel the sweat beneath his hat and his shirt.

"I like it."

"Damn Indian blood," Locke replied.

"Street looks clear," Hawkes said. He glanced up. " 'course, if someone wanted to pick us off from the roof there ain't much we could do about that."

"I'm getting slow," Locke said, also looking up now that Hawkes had mentioned the roof, "and sloppy."

"Sounds to me like you did okay."

"Colon was smart to tell me the men I killed were morons," Locke said. "That's why he answered my questions and identified them. He wanted me to know I hadn't faced his best men."

"Still," Hawkes said, shaking his head, "three men . . ."

"Let's go," Locke said. "It's as clear as it's going to get."

On the way to Vestal's general store Locke decided to stop at the gunsmith shop the storekeeper had told him about. Even with Hawkes in town he wanted a backup.

He and the hangman entered the shop. The air was filled with the odor of gunmetal and oil. The man standing behind the counter was slender and in his sixties, and smiled as they entered.

"Mr. Locke, I presume," he said.

"That's right," Locke said, "how did you know?"

"I've been expecting you ever since you got to town," the man said. "I figured you'd need another weapon sooner or later."

"Well, you were right, friend," Locke said. "What's your name?"

"Name's Les Williams. Jus' call me Les."

"Les, this is my friend Arlo Hawkes," Locke said. "Hawkes is the hangman who's going to execute Ignacio Colon."

"A pleasure to meet you," Les said. "I'll be there to see it. What can I help you gents with?"

"I need a backup weapon," Locke said. "Nothing fancy, just something reliable."

"That Peacemaker you're wearin' reliable?" Les asked.

"Definitely."

"I got somethin' for you, then." Les opened his gun case from behind, reached in, and brought out a Peacemaker similar to Locke's. "I can see just by lookin' at yours that you like a short barrel. This one's five and a half inches, with pearl grips. It was originally single-action, but I've converted it into a double-action weapon."

Locke stepped forward and took the gun. The pearl handle was a little fancy for him, but he knew the weapon to be a reliable model, and this gun looked well cared for.

"I'll take it," Locke said.

"It's yours," Les said, "and I'm proud to have you carry it." The older man looked at Hawkes. "What about you, big feller? You want somethin' to go along with that Winchester of yours?"

"I don't usually carry a sidearm—" Hawkes started, but Locke interrupted him.

"It's free, Arlo. The town is supplying whatever we need."

"A free gun?" Hawkes said.

"That's right," Les confirmed.

"Well, hell, then show me what you got."

Les studied Hawkes for a moment, then said, "I think I got just the thing for you, big feller."

He reached into his case and came out with a huge handgun.

"What is that?" Hawkes asked.

"This is a .44 Army Colt with an eight-inch barrel. It's single-action, but a very effective weapon and will probably fit your hand perfectly."

Hawkes stepped forward, laid his Winchester on the top of the counter and took the gun from the gunsmith's hand.

"How's it look?" Hawkes asked Locke, turning with the weapon in his hand.

"It fits you."

"I'll take it," the big hangman said to the gunsmith. "You sure know how to fit a gun to the man, friend."

"I'll throw in a box of shells for each, and gun belts, if you want them."

"Not for me," Locke said. "I don't need to wear another gun belt. I'll just tuck it in my belt."

"Me, too," Hawkes said. "Never did feel comfortable with a gun belt around my waist."

"Then take 'em and use 'em in good health," Les said. He turned around and took down two boxes of shells from the shelf behind him.

Each man picked up his weapon and shells and loaded his new weapon. That done they emptied the boxes and stuffed their pockets with shells.

"You make up a bill of sale, Les, and I'll have the Town Council reimburse you."

"It's my pleasure to supply you with these weapons, gentlemen."

"I appreciate that, Les," Locke said, "but I'm still going to have the town pay you."

"I'll getcha your bill o' sale, then."

"You got yourself a sweet deal here, John," Hawkes said. "What else can we get for free?"

"Well, Arlo," Locke said, "we could get killed for free."

Hawkes made a face. "I knew there'd be a catch."

FORTY-THREE

When Locke entered Vestal's store with Hawkes, Ed Hansen was behind the counter. It was odd, but Locke never thought of it as Hansen's store, just Vestal's. He would have bet anything Vestal thought of it that way, too.

"M-Mr. Locke," Hansen stammered.

"Mr. Hansen," Locke said, "I'd like you to meet Arlo Hawkes."

"Mr. . . . Hawkes?" Hansen said.

"Hello."

"Is he . . ." Hansen started, then stopped short.

"Is he what?" Locke asked.

"I-I don't know—I was going to ask—is he—"

"He's your hangman."

"M-my hangman?" Hansen asked, his eyes wide.

"He's the man who is going to hang Ignacio Colon," Locke said, slowly.

"You know," Hawkes said, "pull the lever? Drop him through the trapdoor?"

"Oh . . . oh, I see," Hansen said, with something akin to relief—except he was still obviously too afraid to feel any genuine relief.

"Where's your partner?" Locke asked. "I want to introduce him to Hawkes."

"Oh, uh, Gordon is in the office. I can take you back—"

At that moment two middle-aged women wearing calico dresses and bonnets entered the store, stopping to stare up in awe at Hawkes.

"Ladies," the big man said. "If I had a hat I'd tip it to you."

Both women tittered. Hawkes had this effect on women, young and old. It often amazed Locke what the big man could get away with when it came to women.

"Locke," he said, "why don't we go on back ourselves and allow Mr. Hansen to take care of these two lovely ladies."

The women tittered some more and Locke said, "Good idea. We'll just take ourselves back, Hansen."

"I don't think—" Hansen started, but Locke and Hawkes were already on their way.

"Come!" Vestal called out in reply to the knock at his door. When the door opened and Locke entered, followed closely by Hawkes, Vestal sat back in his chair and caught his breath. The office was small, and it became that much smaller with the big hangman in it.

"Locke," he said, finding his voice. "What can I do for you?"

"I wanted you to meet your hangman, Vestal," Locke said. "Arlo Hawkes."

Vestal looked Hawkes up and down, which was no easy feat. He took in the broad shoulders, the hairless chest—

which was evident because Hawkes could never find shirts that would close all the way—the huge hands which dwarfed the Winchester he was holding, and the long-barreled gun tucked into his belt. The man's Indian features were undeniable, made even more striking by the piercing blue eyes.

"Mr. Hawkes," Vestal said.

"Sir."

"Have you seen our gallows?"

"Not yet," Hawkes said. "I'm looking forward to testing it."

"Has Mr. Locke explained the entire situation to you?"

"Oh, yes," Hawkes said, "I know exactly what we're facing."

Vestal leaned back in his chair again. It seemed to be the only way he could get any air. Locke himself was a strongly built big man, but even he seemed undersized by comparison.

"You two know each other?" he asked. "You've worked together before?"

"Sure have," Locke said.

Vestal nodded.

"I see."

"Here's a bill of sale for two extra guns and ammo we got from the gunsmith shop you sent me to. I assume you'll have it taken care of?"

Vestal accepted the piece of paper from Locke and set it down on his desk.

"All of the merchants are being . . . reimbursed where

necessary. Hopefully, some of them will simply donate their wares to the cause."

"What cause is that?" Hawkes asked.

"Why, the cause of justice, of course."

"Of course . . ."

"I don't want the people of this town to be sorry you hired me."

"No," Vestal said, "of course not."

"I'm going to take Hawkes over to see the gallows, and meet the judge."

"An excellent idea," Vestal said. "By all means introduce him to the judge. Mr. Hawkes, a pleasure to meet you."

"And you, sir," Hawkes said, politely.

He opened the door and stepped out, suddenly leaving the room a normal size again.

"An impressive man," Vestal said. "Is he good at his job?"

"His job?" Locke said. "Oh, he's very good. He'll also come in handy in a fight."

"I would imagine so. And you expect a fight tomorrow, do you?"

"If not today," Locke said. "I think it's unavoidable."

"Just the two of you against Colon's bandidos?"

"If need be," Locke said, "but I might have another gun to stand with us later on today."

"And who would that be?"

"I don't even know that," Locke said. "Hawkes has set it up as a surprise."

"Well then," Vestal said, "I look forward to being surprised."

"Yes," Locke said, "so do I." He touched the brim of his

hat and stepped from the room, closing the door behind him.

Vestal wished he could see the look on Judge Tinsley's face when he met Arlo Hawkes, the hangman.

FORTY-FOUR

"**T**hat man's got snake oil salesman written all over him," Hawkes said when they were outside. Hansen was still helping the two ladies who had come in, so they left without saying a word to him. The two women looked at Hawkes and tittered one last time.

"Don't I know it."

"And you took this job, anyway?"

"It was time. I needed a job that wasn't easy."

"Seems to me you got what you were looking for, but at least you've done all right."

"Have I?"

"Didn't you tell me you gunned three men?"

"They weren't much," Locke said. "Maybe I'm not much anymore."

"Locke, if you have doubts why don't you just go back to Mexico?"

"That's not an option."

"Look, Tombstone was a long time ago, Locke. What happened then—"

"Don't!"

The big man put up one hand. "Sorry, I know you don't like to talk about that."

"No, I don't."

"Well, then, lets go take a look at my gallows."

Locke introduced Hawkes to Gavin James and then watched the two men inspect the nearly completed gallows. They discussed the finer points of erecting a scaffold, talked about the trapdoor mechanism, which James assured him would be functional, even though it would not be conventional.

The two men came down off the scaffold back to where Locke was standing.

"Well, I'm satisfied," Hawkes said. "A nice, solid job."

"Thank you, sir," James said. "It'll be ready for testing first thing in the morning. I assure you."

"I believe you," Hawkes said, "and I'll be here to try it out."

Hawkes's tone was nothing but pleasant, but Locke could see Gavin James swallow at the thought of not being there and ready when Hawkes showed up.

"Do you need a rope?"

"I do this for a living, Mr. James," Hawkes said. "I have a rope."

"Of course," James said, "of course you do. I meant no offense."

"And none taken." Hawkes put out his hand and James reluctantly handed his over. "Nice job."

"Thank you."

"Let's go meet the judge, Arlo," Locke said, "and then I'll get you checked into the hotel."

*   *   *

The judge agreed to see Locke when his clerk announced his presence. He was surprised, however, when Locke walked in with Hawkes in tow.

"Mr. Locke," Tinsley said, "I was not aware that you had someone with you." The look on his face said that his clerk would pay for that oversight.

"Judge, I thought you'd like to meet the man who is going to put the noose around Ignacio Colon's neck."

The judge stared at Hawkes in obvious surprise.

"This is the hangman?"

"Arlo Hawkes," Locke said, "a very experienced hangman, at that."

"Really?" The disbelief was now plain on the jurist's face.

Arlo Hawkes gave the judge a wide smile, not saying a word.

"Does he speak?" the judge asked.

"When he has something to say," Locke said.

The judge studied Hawkes dubiously, then asked Locke, "Could we talk alone a moment?"

"I don't see why not," Locke said. "Do you, Arlo?"

Hawkes shook his head and withdrew from the room, the smile never leaving his face.

"The man's an Indian," Tinsley said.

"Half Apache."

"I can't have an Apache hanging a white man in my town."

"When did Colon become a white man?" Locke asked. "He's Mexican."

The judge blinked and said, "Yes, of course, but . . . is this Indian fellow addled?"

"He's fine, Judge," Locke said. "You insulted him, so he chose not to speak to you, but he's a bona fide hangman. I've worked with him before."

"You've officiated at hangings before?" Judge Tinsley asked. "I thought this was something new for you."

"It is," Locke said, "but I've been to hangings before."

"I can't quite believe—I mean, he looks like a savage."

"He's not," Locke said, "and he is also good with a gun. I'm probably going to need a capable man or two like that before this is over."

"Well," the judge said, "I can't argue that. Are you getting cooperation from the sheriff?"

"Very little," Locke said.

"I beg your pardon?"

"I found out that the man tripped over an unconscious Colon. That's how he arrested him."

"I fail to see the signific——"

"And so far all he's been willing to do is lock and unlock the cell block so I can talk to the prisoner. He's not going to be very much help tomorrow, is he?"

"I'm sure he'll do his job."

"Which is that?"

"Walking the prisoner to the gallows."

"I guess he can do that," Locke said, "if he doesn't trip along the way—and the same goes for his deputies."

"Mr. Locke," the judge said, "if you feel you need other men, then get them."

"At your expense?"

"My—"

"I mean the council's . . . the town's."

"We're paying you, sir," the judge said, "supplying you with the things you need, as well as room and board. I don't think we can be expected to—"

"Don't worry, Judge," Locke said, cutting the man off, "all you have to pay Hawkes is his fee as hangman. As for backing my play, he'll do that for fun."

"Fun?"

"And I expect extra help this evening from a friend who will probably do it for the same reason."

"Just who might that be?"

Locke smiled and said, "I think we'll both find that out around the same time. The gallows is almost ready. Hawkes will test it in the morning."

"That's fine," Tinsley said. "I can see the scaffold from my window."

"So can Colon."

"Good," the judge said. "Maybe he'll have time to think about the actions that put him in this position."

"I can guarantee, Judge, that all he's thinking about is escaping."

"I'm sure you and your, uh, friends will see that doesn't happen."

"Oh, definitely," Locke said, "Colon is going to hang tomorrow. No doubt about it."

"That's, uh, good to hear."

"Is it?"

The judge didn't know how to respond to that question, but he didn't have to, as Locke turned and left his office.

FORTY-FIVE

"So these are the men you're working for?" Arlo Hawkes asked.

"Yes."

Locke and Hawkes were in the Main Street Hotel bar. Hawkes had a beer in front of him, Locke a cup of coffee. It was midday and Locke had already spoken with Colon, greeted and briefed Hawkes, eaten with him and introduced him to everyone involved . . . or maybe not everyone.

"Why do they call this the Main Street Hotel?" Hawkes asked, "when the street that runs down the center of town is called Front Street?"

"You know," Locke said, "I never thought to ask."

"I picked up one of these," Hawkes said. From his back pocket he pulled a folded copy of the *Fredericksburg Front Page* and set it down on the table.

"Ah."

"Quite a story this woman wrote," the hangman said. "She's impressed with you."

"She's trying to sell newspapers," Locke said. "I suppose I owe her an interview."

"You don't give interviews."

"It was a barter." Locke explained about needing someone to print the invitations.

"I guess we're expecting a helluva turnout tomorrow."

"Yes," Locke said, "townspeople, families of the victims of Ignacio Colon and his men . . . oh, and don't forget Colon's men."

"To get him out of town," Hawkes said. "How many do you expect?"

"At least fourteen," Locke said, "maybe more."

"How many more?"

"I can't even venture a guess."

Hawkes took a swallow of beer thoughtfully. Locke watched him, knowing what was coming. He decided just to wait.

"John, can I say something?"

"Go ahead."

"This might not have been the right job to take to prove you still had sand."

"Is that what I'm doing?"

"I think so."

Now it was Locke who sipped his coffee carefully before replying.

"Let's say you're right," he said. "It's a little too late to do anything about it now."

"You could quit," Hawkes said, "move on. Look for another job."

"An easier one?"

"Why not?"

"Would you quit, Arlo?"

"John," Hawkes said, "I'm thirty-two years old, and I'm in my prime."

"And I'm fifty," Locke said, "well past mine."

"I didn't mean—"

"Yes, you did mean it," Locke said, "and you're right. I am past it, but I'm not dead . . . hell, I'm not even done."

"You're better than any five men I know combined," Hawkes said.

"Thanks."

"You got nothing to prove as far as I'm concerned," the big man went on. "Why not just leave?"

"Because if I leave," Locke said, "if I don't see this through, then I really am done. I might as well be dead. Also, if I leave now these people can't protect themselves."

"Fine," Hawkes said.

"If you want out I'll understand, Arlo."

"No, Locke," Hawkes said, "I don't want out. What I would like, though, is for you to come up with a plan. Something we can use when the two of us have to face at least fourteen bandidos hell-bent on freeing their leader."

Locke pushed his coffee cup away.

"I think it's time for my beer."

FORTY-SIX

Mendoza was surprised to see the gringo riding out so close to dusk. He usually made a point of coming out earlier.

"Hernando," he said, "bring him to me. He must have something of great importance to say to be out this late."

"Sí, Carlos."

There were several campfires burning and Mendoza was sitting by one alone. The rest of the men were scattered around the other fires, which suited the temporary leader of the group. He wanted to talk to the gringo alone, anyway. It was time to get some things straight.

"Carlos," the gringo said, walking to the fire with Hernando Juarez right behind him.

"Hernando," Carlos said, "leave us. Señor Vestal and I need to talk."

"But Carlos—"

"Hernando! Go!"

Juarez slunk away to join the other men, insulted.

"Carlos," Vestal said, "you're going to need more men for tomorrow."

"And why is that, Señor Vestal?"

"I met Locke's hangman today," the storekeeper said. "He's formidable, as Locke himself has proven to be."

"But, he is the hangman, no?"

"He's also backing Locke's play."

Mendoza gave an unconcerned shrug.

"Two men."

"They're expecting one more."

"Three, then, against all of us."

Vestal looked around. At normal strength Ignacio Colon's bandidos numbered fourteen. It looked to him like they'd added about six more.

"We have enough men for the job, señor."

"I say you need more, Carlos."

"But señor," Mendoza said, "I am the leader here, not you. I decide how many men I need."

"You forget," Vestal said, "you're only the leader as long as Ignacio is in jail—and I'm his partner."

"His partner," Mendoza repeated, "not mine."

Vestal moved closer to Mendoza.

"It doesn't have to be that way, Carlos," Vestal said.

"What do you mean?"

"I mean," Vestal said, "it could be you and me as partners."

"You want to be partners with me?"

"I'm just saying . . . if Ignacio was to hang . . . you know . . . we could continue the arrangement that he and I had."

Mendoza stared at Vestal just long enough to make the storekeeper nervous.

"You want me to let Ignacio hang?"

"I'm not saying that," Vestal said, hurriedly, "I'm just saying if . . ."

"I do not think I would want to be partners with you, Señor Vestal."

"Why not?"

"Truthfully," Mendoza said, "I would not be able to trust you. And in the end, I would probably have to kill you."

"Listen, you greaser," Vestal said, tightly, "I've tolerated your disrespect ever since Ignacio was arrested, but no more—" Vestal stopped short when he felt the sharp end of a knife prodding him below the belt.

"Señor Vestal," Mendoza said, menacingly, "the respect you receive from me must be earned, comprende? I do not give my respect lightly, especially to a gringo."

"Carlos," Vestal said, speaking carefully now, "I only rode out here to warn you—"

"You rode out here to tell me what to do," Mendoza said, rotating the knife so that the point dug deeper into Vestal, "and to call me names. You, señor, came out here to disrespect me! For that, I should cut off your cojones."

"Carlos, n-no—"

"It is getting dark, señor," Mendoza said. "I would not want you to fall off your horse on the way back to town." With his other hand Mendoza waved Juarez over again.

"Sí, Carlos?"

"Take Señor Vestal to his horse. His visit is ended." Mendoza removed the knife from Vestal's groin. "You tell

Ignacio to be ready, señor. We will come when he is out in the open."

"I-I'll tell him," Vestal said, staring at Mendoza with hatred in his eyes. Bad enough he'd had to take crap from Ignacio Colon all these months, he wasn't going to take it from a common bandido, as well. When Ignacio was safely away from the gallows, and from Fredericksburg, Vestal would have a talk with him, and Mendoza would pay.

"This way, señor," Juarez said, as Mendoza sheathed his knife.

"What was that about, Carlos?" Juarez asked, after Vestal had ridden off.

"Señor Vestal wanted to warn us that we would have to face three men when we ride into town tomorrow, and not one."

"Tres? Did he think that would keep us from rescuing Ignacio?"

"The gringo has cojones like pebbles, Hernando," Mendoza said. "Without Ignacio, he is nothing."

"Without Ignacio," Juarez said, "we are all nothing, no?"

Mendoza turned on Hernando Juarez and slapped him soundly across the face.

"No!" he snapped. "I do not need Ignacio in order to be someone."

"But . . . we are going to rescue him, are we not?"

"Mañana," Mendoza said, "we will ride into Fredericksburg."

Juarez withdrew, rubbing his cheek.

FORTY-SEVEN

In the time it took Locke to drink his beer Hawkes had three more and showed few if any effects. He didn't know what kind of pleasure the big man got out of the drinking if it didn't affect him. Although he never had Arlo Hawkes's capacity for drinking even when he was younger, Locke had done his share of drinking and was in no position to comment.

However, by the time he got to the bottom of his own beer he had an idea.

"Okay," he said to Hawkes, "how about this?"

He outlined his plan, with the big man listening intently and nodding.

"What do you think?"

"You just came up with that?"

"Yes."

Hawkes nodded and gave it some thought.

"What do you think?"

"I think it works unless we're totally outnumbered," Hawkes said. "You say there's fourteen, so if they come in at more we're okay—but what if they come in forty or fifty strong?"

"Then we're in trouble, but I don't think Colon's got that many followers, and I don't think the ones he has are going to spend their money hiring that much more help. Besides, we're dealing with a great deal of arrogance, here. Colon and his men won't think they'll need that much help."

"Colon say that?"

"Just about," Locke said. "He's sure that he's not going to hang, no matter what happens."

"Why would he be that sure?"

"That's a good question," Locke said. "I think it's more than just his arrogance."

"Like what?"

"Ever since I got here I've had the feeling there are a lot of things I'm not being told."

"Well, do you know anyone who might be able to tell you?"

Locke played with his empty mug for a moment, spinning it around and around, before answering.

"I think I just might."

"Oh, my," Nina Ballinger said when she saw Locke enter the newspaper office with Arlo Hawkes behind him. Augustus was not around, since she'd put her final edition to bed.

"Miss Ballinger, this is Arlo Hawkes. Hawkes, the newspaper editor Nina Ballinger."

"A pleasure, Miss Ballinger," Hawkes said. If he'd been wearing a hat he would have tipped it.

"I thought you'd be very interested to meet Hawkes," Locke told her.

"Well," she said, "aside from the obvious reasons, why?"

"He's the man who's going to execute Ignacio Colon. He's the hangman."

Nina stared at Hawkes for a few moments, then looked at Locke with a knowing expression on her face.

"You want something."

"What?"

"You want something from me," she said, nodding her head. "And you want to trade for it."

"Well—"

"Why should I trust you when you went back on your promise of an interview?"

"You broke your promise to this lovely lady?" Hawkes asked.

"You keep quiet," Nina said to the big man.

"Huh?" Hawkes looked puzzled.

"You're with him," she said. "I'm not letting either of you put something over on me this time."

"Nina," Locke said, "I just want to ask—"

"I want my interview."

"I gave you—"

"Yeah, yeah, I know," she said, "you gave me an interview and I asked all the wrong questions. I don't buy that as an excuse, Locke. I want my interview."

"Tell you what," Locke said. "If I live through tomorrow, you get your interview."

She stared at him. "That's a morbid bargain if I ever heard one."

"Look," he said, "I need your help to get through tomorrow."

"My help? What do you want me to do, pick up a gun? Stand with you against Colon's bandidos?"

"Not quite," Locke said. "I want to use your knowledge of the people in this town."

"To do what?"

"I think I know what's going on, what's not being said, but I have to ask a few questions to be sure."

"You want to ask *me* a few questions."

"That's right."

She folded her arms across her chest and stared at him, then at Hawkes, who was still looking somewhat bemused.

"You have to buy me dinner tonight," she said. "You can ask me whatever questions you like over an expensive dinner at The Dexter House."

"Agreed."

"And he has to come, too." She pointed at Hawkes.

"I wanted to show him The Dexter House, anyway," Locke said. "He'll be there."

"And I want an interview—"

"I already said—"

"—from him."

Locke turned and looked at Hawkes.

"I think an interview with a hangman would be very interesting," Nina said.

"That's up to Arlo," Locke said.

"What do you say?" Nina asked.

Hawkes laughed and said, "I like this lady, John. Sure, Miss Ballinger, you can interview me—and you don't even have to wait to see if I die. I'll talk to you before tomorrow's hanging."

"There you go," Locke said to Nina. "Now are we agreed?"

She thought a moment, then said, "Agreed."

"Then let's go—"

"Oh, no, I'm not going looking like this," she said.

"I think you look just fine," Hawkes said. A look passed between him and Nina that Locke couldn't miss.

"I want to take a bath and change. Meet me at The Dexter House at seven."

"Seven," Locke said. "Okay."

"Now get out of here so I can close up shop and go home."

"See you at seven, ma'am," Hawkes said.

Locke and Hawkes went outside onto the boardwalk and Nina closed and locked the door behind them.

"That's a fine looking woman, Locke," Hawkes said. "She ain't wearin' your brand, is she?"

"Hell no," Locke said. "She sure does like you, though."

"What makes you say that?"

"She didn't take a bath and change her clothes when she had dinner with me last night."

FORTY-EIGHT

After leaving the newspaper office they had gone back down the street to where Gavin James and his helpers were still working, to discuss Locke's idea.

"Can you make these modifications?" Locke asked, after explaining his plan.

"I can," James said, "and it won't add that much more time to the job. What you're asking is fairly simple."

"Well," Hawkes said, "at least your part is."

"Did I mention that I'm also a fair hand with a gun?" James asked.

"That's good," Locke said, "but this is not something we would ask a bunch of shopkeepers to do, Mr. James."

"I realize that. Would it help you to know that I ran against Sheriff Horrigan for his job in the last election—and I was more qualified?"

"Well," Locke said, "that wouldn't surprise me, at all."

"After I lost, I decided to just open up shop as a carpenter," James said. "So if you're willing to let me help, I'll be there."

"Do you have a gun?"

"Of course," James said. "A pistol and a rifle."

Locke looked at Hawkes.

"We need more guns, John."

"All right, then," Locke said. "We have another friend who may be riding into town tonight, so that makes four of us. Oh, and the bartender—what was his name— Ames?"

"Ben Ames," James said. "He's more than the bartender over there, he owns the place."

"He also offered to help," Locke said, "so that would be five."

"Odds are getting worse for the bandits by the minute," Hawkes said.

"If you know anyone else who's interested in seeing that this hanging goes off as scheduled come over to the hotel and let me know tonight," Locke said.

"I'll do it," James said, "but what about the sheriff?"

"I don't know how much help he'll be," Locke said, "or his deputies."

"Looks to me like we should find out," Hawkes said.

"Maybe you're right. Guess you should meet the local lawman, anyway."

They went directly from the scaffold to the sheriff's office. Horrigan was seated behind his desk. His eyes widened when he saw Arlo Hawkes.

"Sheriff," Locke said, "I want you to meet Colon's hangman, Arlo Hawkes."

"You're the hangman?" Horrigan asked, standing.

"That's right," Hawkes said. "I'll be testing the scaffolding and the trapdoor tomorrow morning. It's usually customary for the sheriff to be there."

"Don't worry, I'll be there," Horrigan said. He looked at Locke. "You really think this is going to happen? Colon seems pretty confident."

"Too confident," Locke said, "and not only do I think it's going to happen, I'm going to make it happen. What I want to know from you is, how much help can I expect?"

"Uh, like I said, I'll be there to walk him out," Horrigan said.

"Where will you be when his men come riding into town with their guns blazing?" Locke asked. "And where will your deputies be?"

"I can't speak for my deputies," Horrigan said. "I have three, they're all young men and relatively untested."

"And you?"

Horrigan had remained standing and now shifted his feet.

"I know you don't think much of me as a lawman, Mr. Locke," he said, finally. "It's true I caught Colon almost by accident, but I caught him, and I don't want to see him get away."

"That wouldn't be good for you," Hawkes said.

"N-no, it wouldn't," Horrigan said. "I think he's embarrassed by the fact that it was me who captured him, so you're right, Mr. Hawkes. It would not be good for me if he got away."

"Can you use that gun, Sheriff?" Locke asked.

The sheriff looked down at the gun in his holster, and then back at Locke.

"I'm no gunman, Mr. Locke," Horrigan said, "but I can fire the weapon."

"Then I guess the question becomes . . . *will* you use it?"

"No matter what you think of me," Horrigan said, "I'll do my job."

"Sheriff," Locke said, "I realize there are things going on in this town that I don't know about. There are sides that have been drawn and I have no idea who is standing where. But I promise you one thing . . . I'm going to find out."

"W-what do you mean?"

"I mean Colon is entirely too confident that he's not going to hang," Locke said again. "That means he's working with someone in this town who he thinks is going to save him."

"And who do you think that might be?"

Locke studied the lawman for a moment.

"Maybe you're as innocent as you seem, and then again, maybe you're not," he said, finally. "I'm going to find that out, too. In fact, I'm going to learn everything there is to know about this town, and in the end Colon is going to hang and there are going to be some happy people and some unhappy people."

He turned to leave, Hawkes moving to the door ahead of him. The big man opened the door and stepped out, but Locke turned back to the sheriff and said, "I intend to be one of the happy ones."

FORTY-NINE

When Locke and Hawkes reached The Dexter House later that evening they found Nina Ballinger already seated and waiting. She was wearing a dress that revealed more of her neck, shoulders, and breasts than Locke had seen before, without being wholly immodest.

Hawkes drew looks from most of the other diners as they walked over and sat down across from her. She had taken a table that was against a wall, but the best Locke could do was sit with his left shoulder against it. Hawkes sat next to him, directly across from Nina. Locke had a good view of the entire room despite his angle. Only his vision of the doorway was blocked, and that was by Arlo Hawkes's bulk. He did have room, though, to stretch out his injured leg, which was stiffening up now that it was the end of the day.

"Miss Ballinger," Hawkes said to her, "you look lovely."

"Why, thank you, Mr. Hawkes."

Locke thought if Hawkes was going to start turning on the charm he didn't have much time to hold her attention.

"Before you two start complimenting each other," he said, "I'd like to get down to the heart of the matter."

"Can we order first?" Hawkes asked. "I'm hungry."

"You're always hungry," Locke said. "Sure, go ahead and order."

"How about three pot roast dinners?" Nina Ballinger suggested. "It'll be easier that way and it's the special tonight."

"Fine with me," Locke said, looking around the room. There was no sign of either Judge Tinsley or Gordon Vestal. However, the tables were full, and maybe the two leaders of the Town Council would be dining later—if they had not already.

They ordered their dinners and while they were waiting Nina Ballinger said, "All right, Mr. Locke. What is it you would like to ask me?"

"Miss Ballinger—"

"I thought you were going to call me Nina . . . John?"

"Fine . . . Nina. I get the distinct feeling that not everyone in town wants to see Ignacio Colon hang. Is that true?"

"Well . . . I don't know who wouldn't, but you're probably right. There might be a person or two who think he's . . . a romantic figure."

"No, that's not what I mean," Locke said. "I'm talking about someone in power, someone who might be able to keep Colon from being executed."

"Like who?"

"Well . . . Judge Tinsley, for instance."

"But the judge sentenced him to hang," Nina said. "Why would he do anything to change that decision?"

"I don't know," Locke said, "but Colon's entirely too

sure that he's not going to hang. The only reason I can think of is that he might be depending on someone here in town to save him."

"He's probably just sure his men will save him," Hawkes said.

"You've dealt with outlaws, Arlo, you tell me—is there honor among thieves?"

"What's he mean?" Nina asked.

"He means that there's got to be someone among his band who would like to see him dead, maybe somebody who wants to take over."

"So they may not come to save him tomorrow?"

"That would be the ideal solution," Locke said, "but no. I think they'll be here. And I also think there's someone from town in contact with them maybe passing along information."

Nina thought a moment, then said, "Couldn't that be how they learned about you, and sent someone to try and kill you? There's an . . . an informer in town?"

"Exactly."

"John, I know you," Hawkes said. "You wouldn't think that without having an opinion about who it is."

"My opinion may not hold much weight," Locke said. "I haven't had much personal contact with the other members of the council, so I'd guess either the judge or Gordon Vestal."

"Vestal? He's one of the loudest of the men calling for Ignacio Colon's execution."

"Might be an act."

The waiter came with their pot roast, and they each had a moment to think while he set the plates down.

"Gordon Vestal," Nina said, when the waiter was gone. "Why would he be in league with Colon?"

"I don't know," Locke said. "Maybe there's a profit in it for him. He strikes me as the type of man who is solely interested in making money."

"Well, you've got that part right, anyway."

Locke looked over at Hawkes's plate and saw that the man was already half finished with his meal. He was feeding it into his mouth in chunks twice as big as the ones he was cutting, and three times the size of the ones Nina was eating.

Feeling himself being watched, Hawkes looked at Locke, and then back down to his plate. He seemed to realize what he had been doing, and that it would not look good in front of the lovely Nina Ballinger to wolf down his food. In order to slow himself down, he reached for the beer he had ordered and sipped it. Locke and Nina were both having water with their meals.

"I need your opinion, Nina," Locke said. "Do you think it would be Vestal, or the judge?"

"My opinion?" she asked. "Why is my opinion of any value?"

"Because you have your finger on the pulse of this town, and you know these men much better than I do."

"And you're intelligent," Hawkes added.

"Thank you, Mr. Hawkes."

The glances Hawkes and Nina were tossing across the table at each other were getting hotter. Locke needed to finish before they started to sizzle.

"Nina?"

"John, I . . . oh, very well. If you're giving me a choice between Vestal and the judge, I'd have to say Vestal."

"Why?"

"Because it would have been easy for the judge to find Colon innocent and set him free."

"Would it have been easy?" Locke asked. "How much evidence was there?"

"Eye witnesses to several murders," Nina said.

"Then Tinsley would have looked mighty bad letting him off."

"I suppose." She put down her fork and stared at him. "Now I'm not sure what I think. Are you two actually going to go through with this?"

"I have to go through with it," Locke said. "As for Arlo, well, he's just the hangman. He doesn't have to do anything else, if he doesn't want to."

"I wouldn't let you face those bandidos alone, my friend," Hawkes said.

"That's very noble—" Nina said.

"Well—" Hawkes started, sheepishly, but she didn't let him finish.

"—but it's stupid."

"What?" Hawkes asked.

"Do either of you think this is impressing me?" she asked. "Two against . . . I don't know how many. How stupid is that? You're just going to get yourself killed." She glared at Locke. "Why did you take this job in the first place? If the town wants Colon hanged why don't you let them do it?"

"That's what they hired me for," Locke said.

"But once you realized you'd get no help from any-one—" she started to ask, then suddenly stopped.

"Nina?" Locke said.

"My God!" she breathed. She had turned her head to her left and was staring at the doorway. "That man looks positively ill. How can he even be standing?"

Hawkes turned to look, and Locke had to lean forward in order to look past the big man. A slight, fair-haired man in a gambler's black suit had entered the restaurant. Nina was right, he looked like death warmed over.

"He—he seems to be coming over here," she said.

Sure enough the man had spotted them and was walk-ing toward their table. Other diners glanced at him, but his condition was such that they looked away quickly.

The man reached their table and looked down at the three of them. His flesh was pale, his eyes red-rimmed. He seemed barely able to stand.

"Figured ah'd find you two at the best restaurant in town," he said, in a slight southern accent. He looked at Nina and said, "Pahdon me, ma'am."

"I-I—" she stammered.

"Nina Ballinger," Locke said, "meet our friend, John Henry Holliday."

"John Henry—" she repeated.

Hawkes looked up at the man and said, "Hello, Doc."

FIFTY

"Doc Holliday?" Nina Ballinger asked. "*The* Doc Holliday?"

"At your service, ma'am," Doc said, tipping his hat.

"Join us, Doc?" Locke asked.

"If the lady doesn't mind?"

"Actually," Nina said, pushing her chair back, "I have to be leaving. I need to be up early in the morning to get out an early edition about the hanging."

"Ah'm not scarin' you off, am ah?" Doc asked.

"N-no, of course not, Mr. Holliday," she said. "I-It's a pleasure to meet you."

Hawkes pushed his chair back and said, "I'll walk you home, Nina. We need to discuss when to do my interview."

"Yes, of course we do," she said. "That would be fine, Arlo."

"Doc," Hawkes said, putting out his hand, "see you later at the saloon?"

"Which saloon?" the Southerner asked.

"Locke will let you know."

Doc watched as Hawkes left with Nina Ballinger, then turned and took the seat Nina had just vacated.

"I frightened her away," the one-time dentist said.

"I think so."

Doc reached across the table to shake hands with Locke.

"It's been a long time, Locke."

"Tombstone, Doc," Locke said.

"Ah, yes," Doc said. "A volatile time in the history of this great country. You predicted that, I believe?"

"I gave it six months. It took twice as long. How are the Earps, by the way?"

"I saw Wyatt a short time ago," Doc said. "He has suffered some setbacks, but remains in good spirits."

"And how have you been?"

Doc produced a white handkerchief at that moment, coughed into it, stole a peek at the contents, and then tucked the handkerchief away.

"I believe I am defying all odds, or so the doctors tell me."

"You don't look good, Doc."

Doc smiled wanly and said, "You should see me first thing in the morning. Our mutual friend—who I assume will be busy for the next couple of hours, at least—said you were in need of some help."

"Just a bit."

"Why don't you wait until I get some of that pot roast, and then tell me about it." He waved over a waiter.

Doc worked on his dinner, which meant he cut a few pieces, chewed them for a while, and left the rest. He listened intently while he nibbled. Locke knew from past experience with Doc that consumptives didn't have much of an appetite.

The dentist turned gunman pushed his plate away as Locke finished his story by explaining his plans for tomorrow.

"You got enough men to make that work?" Doc asked.

"I don't honestly know, Doc," Locke said. "I'll know more when I get back to my hotel. Where are you staying?"

"Place down the street," Doc said. "Thought you might be there, too."

"No, Hawkes and I are a few streets away at the Main Street Hotel. Let's walk over there. We'll wait for Hawkes in the hotel bar."

"We need to pay a check?"

"No," Locke said, "I eat for free. Part of my deal."

"Nice deal," Doc said, "if it includes drinkin'."

"It does."

"Then let's get to it."

FIFTY-ONE

They stopped by the scaffolding so Doc could take a look. The carpenter and his helpers must have been at his shop, working on Locke's . . . refinements.

"Looks like your plan could work," Doc said, "if you have enough men, and if the spectators don't get in your way. Sounds like you're going to have a lot of them."

"Yeah, the town's pretty excited about it," Locke said, "and if all the invited family members show up . . . well . . ."

"Let's get that drink."

They walked over to the hotel and Doc waited, dry mouthed—he said—while Locke checked at the front desk for messages.

"Just one," the clerk said, and handed him a piece of paper.

"Thanks."

Locke opened it. It was a note from Gavin James. "Add three men with guns to mine. That makes four."

Locke folded the note and tucked it in his pocket.

"Come on," he said to Doc.

"I thought we were going to drink here."

"I've got a better idea."

Locke took Doc to the saloon owned by Ben Ames, who had offered Locke the use of his shotgun. The place was full, but they managed to get two spaces at the polished mahogany bar.

"Hey, Mr. Locke," Ames greeted. "What can I get you?"

"Whiskey for my friend," Locke said.

"And you?"

"A cup of coffee."

"Comin' up."

"On the wagon?" Doc asked.

"It's a long story."

"Part of it take place in Mexico?"

"You heard?"

"From a mutual friend."

Ames returned with both drinks.

"Good sir, you are a lifesaver," Doc said. He knocked back the whiskey in one movement. "Please bring another."

"He with you?" Ames asked Locke.

"Ben Ames," Locke said, "meet my friend, Doc Holliday."

"D-Doc?"

"The same."

"Drink's comin' up, sir."

Locke sipped his coffee while Ames poured Doc another drink.

"Ben, you made me an offer when we first met. You remember what it was?"

"My shotgun, you mean?" Ames asked. "The offer still stands."

"I need you to stand with me and Doc."

"With Doc Holliday and you?" Ames asked, excitedly.

"That's right," Locke said, "but I've got to warn you, we're dealing with fifteen or twenty of Colon's bandidos."

"Uh, is it just gonna be us three?" Ames asked.

Locke explained to Ames about Arlo Hawkes, Gavin James, and several other men he hadn't met yet.

"Sounds like half a dozen against twenty," Ames said, dubiously.

"They're outnumbered," Doc said to Ames. "Just imagine, my friend, the stories folks will tell about you."

"About me?"

"About the time you stood with Doc and Locke," Doc Holliday said, pushing his glass over to the man.

"Wow," Ames said, refilling Doc's glass.

"Yeah, they'll tell stories after you're dead, too, Ames," Locke warned. "I don't want you to agree unless you really know what you're up against, and only if you can handle it."

"Mr. Locke, I can handle a shotgun, and I'll stand with you. I won't run when the going gets rough."

"Okay, then," Locke said.

"Have a drink on it, Mr. Ames."

"Call me Ben, Doc," the bartender said, pouring himself a drink.

"Drink up, Ben," Doc said. "The night is young, and tomorrow we may die."

"Not if I can help it," Locke said, draining his coffee cup.

They agreed that Ames would meet them at Locke's hotel in the morning with his shotgun. After Doc had a few more drinks they left and walked back to Locke's hotel bar. When they got there Hawkes was standing at the bar with a mug of beer.

"Time for your one, John?" the big man asked.

"Sure, why not?"

Doc agreed to have a beer, as well, so Hawkes ordered three more from the bartender and then handed them out.

"Here's to tomorrow," Doc said. "Nothin' makes you feel so alive as starin' death in the face."

They all drank and then Hawkes asked, "That what you felt after the O.K. Corral, Doc? Alive?"

"Definitely."

"And the Earps?"

"Wyatt was angry," Doc said, "and after Morg was killed, kind of went crazy. Virgil just always seems to be Virgil."

Doc put his mug on the bar and ordered a whiskey.

"Not much going on here," he said, when he had his drink. "I think I'll go back and see our friend Ben, maybe play some cards. Hawkes?"

"You need me to keep you out of trouble?"

Doc smiled and said, "I can keep myself out of trouble . . . if I want to."

"I think I'll stay here, then."

"Locke, see you both in the mornin'," Doc said.

"Doc." Locke was still working on his one beer, and raised the half-filled mug to his friend. "It's good to see you again, amigo."

Doc touched the brim of his hat and left the bar.

"What do you think, Arlo?"

"I've always thought Doc had one foot in the grave, Locke," Hawkes said.

"And now?"

Hawkes picked up the fresh beer the bartender had brought him, taking a moment to collect his thoughts.

"I think he's got both feet in it now," he said, finally. "He's just too damn stubborn to lie down."

FIFTY-TWO

While Locke was finishing his beer Gordon Vestal walked into the sheriff's office.

"Take a break, Ray," Vestal said. "I want to talk to the prisoner."

"Mr. Vestal, I don't think I should—"

"You want to stay sheriff of Fredericksburg, Horrigan?"

"Yes, sir, I do, but—"

"Then get out! Don't make me say it again."

Horrigan stared at Vestal for a few moments, then shook his head, grabbed his hat, and left the office.

Vestal let himself into the cell block.

"We got problems, Ignacio," he said.

"Señor Vestal," Colon said, flashing his gold smile. "What a pleasure."

"Never mind that," Vestal said, approaching his cell and fumbling through the keys. "Which one of these opens your cell?"

"What are you doing, señor?"

"I'm letting you out, Colon," Vestal said. "Everything we've worked for is about to be ruined and I can't let that happen."

"But I will be free tomorrow, señor," Colon said, "as soon as my men come."

"Your men may not be coming," Vestal said. "I talked with Carlos today, and he likes being the leader a little too much."

"What do you mean?"

"I mean Mendoza just might let you swing tomorrow." Vestal tried a key, discarded it, and tried another. "And even if they do come John Locke might stop them."

"I thought you told me that Locke was a drunk?" Colon said, accusingly.

"That was what I heard," Vestal said, "but he didn't act like a drunk when he gunned down three of your men in the street." Another key. "And now he's got help."

"What help?"

"Someone named Hawkes, who is supposed to be the hangman, and I just got word from one of my contacts that Doc Holliday is in town."

"Doc Holliday?"

"Apparently, he's a friend of Locke's."

Colon did not feel quite as confident as he had, but he tried not to let it show.

"But even Doc Holliday, with Locke and this hangman, are only three men."

"Still," Vestal said, "our partnership is too important to risk."

"You mean your profits are too important to risk."

Vestal stood up straight and stared through the bars at Colon.

"Our profits, Ignacio," he said. "Things are not going

according to plan, and there's just too much room for error. Think about it."

The gold in Colon's mouth was nowhere in sight while he thought.

"What about it?" Vestal asked.

"What are you waiting for, you fool?" Colon demanded. "Open the door!"

Colon and Vestal ransacked the sheriff's office until they found the Mexican's guns. He strapped on his bandoleer and his holster, then picked up his rifle.

"All right," he said to Vestal. "I am ready."

"Then get out of town," Vestal said.

"I must finish some business first."

"What business?"

"Your judge," Colon said. "The man who sentenced me to hang. I do not want him to have the chance to do it again."

"Leave the judge to me, then," Vestal said. "You have to get out of town."

"You will kill the judge?" Colon asked, amused.

"I said I'd take care of him!"

"And what about John Locke?" Colon asked. "Apparently El Viudador has not lost his touch, eh?"

"Colon—" Vestal started, but at that moment the door opened and Sheriff Ray Horrigan stepped in.

"What the hell—" he said. He went for his gun, but Ignacio Colon was faster. The bandit leader drew and fired one shot.

FIFTY-THREE

John Locke knew a shot when he heard it.

"Are you sure?" Hawkes asked, as he followed Locke out of the hotel.

They had been in the lobby, Locke about to go to his room. He suspected he was going to see Nina Ballinger. However, when he heard the shot Locke ran from the hotel with Hawkes right behind him.

"I'm sure," he called back to the man trailing behind him.

"How do you know it came from the jail?"

"I don't," Locke said, "but that's the only place I'm going to check, just in case."

The two men ran toward the jail. When they arrived they saw a man lying half in, half out of the doorway.

Locke stopped at the body, allowing Hawkes to step over the man and into the jail to check on Colon. He crouched, turned the man over, and saw Sheriff Horrigan's face.

"Colon's gone," Hawkes said.

Locke looked up at Hawkes. "So is the sheriff." He stood up. "Damn!"

"We didn't pass him in the street," Hawkes said. "He's either keeping to the shadows or . . ."

". . . he's on the way to the livery stable for a horse. Come on."

"Goddamnit!" Gordon Vestal shouted at Ignacio Colon while the man saddled a horse. "Did you have to kill him? The sheriff?"

"You saw him go for his gun," Colon said.

"Yeah, but Christ, man, he was no lawman, he was a damn teacher. You didn't have to kill him. The judge is gonna be after your head now, for sure."

Colon turned and looked at Vestal, the man who had been tipping him off before every robbery he and his bandidos pulled, for a cut of the profits.

"You mean he will want to hang me higher?"

"I mean he'll call in federal help to hunt you down, now," Vestal said. "We're done. Our partnership is dissolved. I don't want anything to do with you ever again."

Colon pulled the cinch tight on the stolen saddle and then turned to face Vestal.

"It is not that easy, señor."

"Hey, I set you free, Ignacio. I've done my part, and now I'm out of it. You're gonna be hunted until the day you die, and I'm not going down with you."

"So we were compañeros, and now we are not?"

"Compan—— what?"

"Partners."

"Hell no, we're not partners anymore."

"Señor," Colon said, showing gold, "there is only one way to dissolve a partnership with Ignacio Colon."

Vestal stared at Colon for a moment, not comprehending what the man was saying. When he did finally understand his eyes widened and he went for the gun that was in a holster beneath his arm. Colon smiled widely, drew his gun, and fired one shot into Vestal's chest, effectively dissolving their partnership forever.

Colon was astride the horse before Vestal's body hit the ground. He turned the horse and rode out the front door. He started in one direction, but saw Arlo Hawkes blocking his path. Then he wheeled the horse around to go in the other direction, and came face to face with John Locke.

"El Viudador!" he shouted.

"Colon," Locke called back. "Dismount and give up."

"Why, so you can hang me?" Colon called out. "I swore I would not be hanged, señor. You must kill me now, or I will kill you."

"It's not going to happen that way, Colon."

"There is no other way it can end, señor," the bandido leader said.

Without any warning Hawkes closed the distance between himself and Ignacio Colon, swung his rifle like a baseball bat, catching Colon in the middle of his back. The Mexican shouted out in pain as he was catapulted from the saddle. When he struck the ground Locke was on him, disarming him and then stepping back.

Colon rolled about on the ground holding his back and cursing in Spanish.

FIFTY-FOUR

"**W**hy did you not just kill me?" Ignacio Colon asked Locke.

"That would have been too easy," Locke said.

"For who, señor?"

Locke stared at Colon through the bars of his cell, where the Mexican was once again incarcerated.

"For both of us, Colon."

The bandido leader was lying on his cot, still holding his back where Hawkes had hit him with his rifle.

"I do not think I will even be able to stand tomorrow," the prisoner complained.

"We'll prop you up."

Colon moaned and rolled over onto his side, grasping his back. Locke left the cell block and locked the door behind him. In the office were Arlo Hawkes, Judge Tinsley, and two of Ray Horrigan's deputies. Also present, as he had come along later after the action was over, was Doc Holliday.

"I can't believe this," Tinsley said. "Horrigan and Vestal dead?"

"Vestal was working with Colon, Judge," Locke said.

"That's why Colon and his men were able to commit so many lucrative robberies. They had inside information."

"It was Vestal who suggested we hire you," the judge said.

"I think that was because he heard stories about my drinking. He must have figured I wouldn't be much of a threat."

Locke remained silent. The two deputies looked at each other for want of something better to do, and Hawkes and Doc exchanged a glance.

"Sometimes," Doc said, finally, "folks just like to pass along nasty rumors, Judge."

The judge walked over to the sheriff's desk and picked up the star which, until a half hour or so before, had been pinned to Ray Horrigan's chest. He looked at the two deputies, who stood up straight, then shook his head and put the badge back down.

"Has anyone talked to Ed Hansen?" the judge asked.

"None of us have," Locke said.

"Someone should tell him his partner's dead," the judge said.

"Someone should probably also find out," Doc Holliday said, "if he was part of the partnership between Vestal and Colon."

Locke looked at his fair-haired friend. Doc had a habit of going right to the heart of the matter.

"Well," Judge Tinsley said, "this won't affect the hanging tomorrow."

"Why should it?" Locke asked. "We're all set."

"I just have to test the scaffolding in the morning," Hawkes said, "and I'll be ready."

Suddenly, they heard the sound of hammering. the judge walked to the door and looked out.

"What are they doing?" he asked. "I thought the gallows was finished?"

"They're making some last minute modifications I requested," Locke said.

"For what reason?"

"I just felt I needed something . . . extra for tomorrow."

The judge stared at him, then said, "Very well. That's your concern. I have only one problem now."

"And what's that?" Locke asked.

The judge picked up the sheriff's badge again and rotated it in his hand.

"We need a new sheriff to walk Colon to the gallows."

The judge looked pointedly at Locke.

"Not me," he said. "I have a job, remember? Appoint one of your eager young deputies, here. If they stood up any straighter and pushed their chests out any further they'd burst their buttons."

Tinsley scowled and said, "They have no experience for this job."

"What experience do they need?" Locke asked. "Give one of them the badge. All they have to do is walk a man to the gallows."

"And then walk away," Holliday said, "alive."

That deepened the judge's scowl.

"Mr. Hawkes—"

"I'm the hangman," Hawkes said, quickly. "To wear a badge would be a conflict of interest."

The judge was becoming increasingly agitated.

"Mr. Holliday, what about you? After your experiences in Tombstone you would be admirably suitable for—"

"I didn't wear a badge in Tombstone," Doc said, coldly, "and I'm not about to start now."

The judge threw up his hands.

"Well, what am I supposed to do, then?" he demanded of anyone who would answer. "Where do I find a qualified man at this late date?"

Locke could still hear Gavin James hammering outside.

"I think I have an idea, Judge."

FIFTY-FIVE

"**M**e?"

Gavin James was the newest member of the group in the sheriff's office.

"Mr. Locke seems to feel you are the logical candidate, Mr. James," Judge Tinsley said. "In light of the fact that you ran against Ray Horrigan in the election, I'm inclined to agree."

Gavin James became angry, an emotion Locke had not seen the man exhibit before.

"Judge, you think I don't know that political pull—your political pull—was used to make sure I lost the last election? And now you want to give me the job?"

"That's history, Mr. James," the judge said. "I do what I think is best for this town."

"Like allying yourself with Mr. Vestal? Who turns out to be connected to Ignacio Colon?"

The judge looked around the room angrily, wondering who had passed the carpenter this information. The two deputies began to fidget. Locke, Hawkes, and Holliday ignored the man's probing gaze.

"It's on the street, sir," James said. "Everyone knows."

The judge cleared his throat, then said, "Be that as it may, this town needs a sheriff and you are now clearly the best candidate." Tinsley held out the badge. "Will you wear this?"

"Just for tomorrow?"

"For the remainder of Ray Horrigan's term," the judge said.

James looked over at Locke, who didn't offer anything in the way of encouragement. The decision was James's alone.

"Well," James said, "the gallows is finished, waiting only for Mr. Hawkes to test it. Once he does that and approves it, I'll accept the job."

"Excellent," Judge Tinsley said. "Mr. Hawkes, would you care to test the scaffolding and trapdoor now?"

"It's dark outside, Judge."

"We'll get some torches," Tinsley said. He looked at the two deputies. "You men see to it that the area of the gallows is well lit."

"And I need a heavy bag," James said. "A sack of potatoes would do."

"See to that, as well," the judge instructed.

"Yes, sir."

"I want my own deputies," James said, after the two deputies had gone.

"What's wrong with them?" Tinsley asked.

"I have nothing against them, but they're too young and inexperienced. There's going to be trouble tomorrow and I intend to back Mr. Locke up. I have several other men willing to help. I'll want them deputized."

"How many?"

"Six."

"Six?" Locke asked.

James turned to him and said, "My two helpers want to keep on helping."

Locke looked at the judge and said, "Six."

"Why not keep those two on and make it eight?" the judge asked.

"They could get killed," Locke said.

"They took the job understanding the risk," Tinsley said. "Why not leave the decision up to them?"

"Why not?" Doc asked before anyone else could. "We could use the extra guns."

This time when James looked at Locke he nodded.

"All right," the new sheriff-to-be said. "I'll give them a choice."

"Let's get to it, then," Hawkes said.

While the others watched, Hawkes mounted the scaffolding and tied a ten pound sack of potatoes to a noose. He explained that normally he would have rigged something heavier, but there was no time. He set the sack down on the trapdoor, then moved to the lever James had rigged.

"Ready?" he called.

"Ready," James said.

He pulled the lever, opening the trapdoor and dropping the sack of potatoes through, so that it dangled by the noose.

"We can't see it," the judge said. "The area beneath

the scaffold is usually in view. Why has it been blocked?"

"That was at my request, Judge," Locke said. "It'll be explained tomorrow."

"Fine," the man said. "You're in charge."

"No," Locke said, "Sheriff James is in charge, but I'll still oversee the hanging."

The judge approached Gavin James and held out the badge. The carpenter-turned-lawman didn't move, and finally the judge grudgingly pinned the badge to his shirt.

"Swear in your deputies, Sheriff," Tinsley said. "I'll see you at the jail in—when's the hanging?"

"In the morning," Locke said. "After Colon's had his last meal."

"Is that really necessary?" the judge asked.

"You sentenced him to hang," Locke pointed out. "That's part of it."

The judge sighed and said, "Very well, but I'll be here at first light."

"Yes, sir," James said.

The judge walked away and James called the two deputies down from the scaffold with their torches.

"Are you two men staying on as deputies?" James asked them.

"Yes, sir," one said.

"You understand what we're up against tomorrow?" Locke asked.

"Yes, sir," the other replied.

"All right, then, let's gather round and I'll tell you

how it's going to go," Locke said. "Sheriff, you can fill your other deputies in come morning."

James was looking down at his badge, but lifted his head and said, "I'm listening."

FIFTY-SIX

Carlos Mendoza rose early the next morning, crouched by the fire, and poured himself a cup of coffee. He was still trying to decide what action he should take this day. He had twenty men to take into Fredericksburg to go against John Locke and Doc Holliday. He discounted the hangman as just a hangman, and also discounted any other help Locke thought he could get from anyone in town. The town was made up mostly of merchants, storekeepers who would be no danger to anyone with a gun in their hands—except maybe themselves.

Freeing Ignacio Colon from the gallows seemed a simple enough task. Just ride in, grab him, and ride out, shooting up a bit of the town—and some of the townspeople—while they were at it. What could be simpler?

What indeed?

"Carlos?"

Mendoza looked up and saw Hernando Juarez looking down at him.

"Hernando."

"Shall I wake the men?"

Mendoza looked into his cup, at the dregs floating on the bottom as if they were tea leaves with a message for him. Abruptly, he tossed them into the fire.

"Sí, Hernando," he said, "wake the men. We ride for Fredericksburg."

Locke woke early, put a new bandage on his wound, dressed, and went out to sit in front of the hotel. He was supposed to meet Hawkes there and have breakfast together. Doc Holliday did not eat breakfast. In fact, he was barely able to get himself out of bed mornings.

"Want us to come and get you, Doc?" Hawkes had asked the night before.

Doc shook his head. "Don't worry, I'll be there for the hangin'—and the action."

"We're not worried, Doc," Locke had said.

Now, as Locke sat in front of the hotel he watched the flow of people filing by, on their way to get a good spot for the hanging. He wondered if the family members of the victims had arrived in town, yet. It was going to be his job to get them onto the viewing stand. He also wondered how many of these innocent bystanders were going to end up getting hurt? Maybe he should have thought about that sooner, but it was too late now. There was no way to keep the town from turning out for this hanging. Maybe he wouldn't be responsible for them getting hurt any more than he was for the man who'd been killed in the Crystal Palace in Dodge five years ago.

He looked down at the early edition of the *Front Page*

he'd grabbed from the hotel lobby. Not only was the hanging on the front page, but also an interview with Arlo Hawkes, the "famed" hangman.

At that moment Hawkes came out of the hotel.

"I'm hungry," he said. "I've got to eat something before I hang a man."

Locke looked up at him.

"Someday you'll have to explain that to me," he said, "or is it in this interview?"

Hawkes leaned over to peer at the paper.

"Wow, she got that in today's edition?" he asked. "When did she have time?"

Locke handed him the paper.

"I was going to ask when and where this interview took place," Locke said, "but never mind. I think I'd rather go and eat."

"Lead the way," the hangman said. "You know all the good places in town."

As they were walking away from the hotel Hawkes said, "And look, she spelled my name right . . ."

John Henry Holliday rolled over in bed and opened his already bloodshot eyes. Good God, another day alive! He not only amazed the doctors, he amazed himself. Sometimes he thought he should just put his gun to his head, or in his mouth, and put himself out of his misery. His single action Colt .45 was hanging on the bedpost, and with a good stretch he could probably reach it. He could have done that right now, but he knew once he started to move he'd begin coughing.

Every morning started that way, with him trying to cough his lungs out. He looked at the night table next to the bed, moving only his eyes. There was a bottle of whiskey there with a couple of mouthfuls still left in it. If he reached for it very slowly—another good stretch would do it—he could get a head start on the day . . . only, damnit, John Locke was waiting for him, wasn't he? That's right, there was supposed to be a hanging this morning. . . .

This day sounded like it might even be as much fun as Tombstone, and he didn't want to miss that, did he? Maybe somebody would even put a bullet or two in him and save him the trouble of dying slowly of consumption.

FIFTY-SEVEN

Locke and Hawkes were halfway through their breakfasts when Nina Ballinger appeared in the café doorway. She spotted them and hurried over.

"Sorry I'm late," she said.

"Late?" Locke asked.

She nodded and sat down next to Hawkes, moving her chair closer to him.

"Yes, Arlo told me where you'd be eating breakfast this morning and invited me to join you."

"How did you know where we'd be having breakfast?" Locke asked Hawkes.

"I told you," the big man answered, "you know where all the best places are."

Nina laughed. "He asked me where to get the best breakfast, and I told him here. He said he was sure you'd found this place already."

Locke stared at Hawkes, who just shrugged.

"Well," Locke said, "if I'd known you were coming I would have waited to order."

"Oh, I just have coffee in the morning," Nina said, rubbing Hawkes's arm up and down.

"That's why I asked for the extra cup," Hawkes said. He freed his arm from her and poured her a cup.

"Ah," Locke said.

"Did you see the paper?" she asked.

"The interview," Locke said. "I saw it."

"Did you read it?"

"Haven't had a chance," he said.

"I think it came out exceptionally well," she said, excitedly. She looked at Hawkes. "Don't you?"

"It's great." Locke knew that Hawkes had not read it yet, either—but then he'd been there when the questions had been asked, hadn't he?

"Today should be very exciting, too," she said.

"You're not going to be there, are you?" Locke asked.

"Of course," she said. "Somebody has to cover it for the paper."

"Send somebody else," he suggested.

"I can't," she said. "I'm the only reporter I have."

Locke put his fork down and looked at Hawkes.

"I tried to talk her out of it last night," he said, "and again this morning. She's very determined."

"Nina—" Locke started.

"John," she said, "this is my job, it's how I make my living."

"There are going to be bullets flying all around," Locke said.

"I'll duck," she said. "Besides, Arlo said you thought maybe Colon's men wouldn't come for him."

"That's just a possibility," Locke said. "Actually, I now think they will come."

"That'll just make a better story, anyway."

"But you'll just have to live through it to write it."

"Locke," she said, "you don't have to try to frighten me. I'm frightened, already."

"But she's still going to come," Hawkes said.

"All right," Locke said to Nina, "I respect you for that."

"Thank you."

"Just don't forget to duck."

Hawkes looked around. "I hope Doc makes it."

"He will."

"Do you think Doc would agree to an interview?" Nina asked.

"I think you should be satisfied with the one you got," Locke said.

"Yes," Hawkes said, "Doc is not a talker."

"I can't believe I have two of the principals from the O.K. Corral here in town and I can't get either one to talk to me about it."

"Two?" Hawkes asked.

"Doc Holliday, and John Locke," she said.

"I wasn't at the O.K. Corral," Locke said, hastily.

"No, but you predicted it."

"I don't know how that story got started!" Locke said. "All I said was . . ."

"Yes?"

Locke sat back and smiled. Nina thought it was the first real smile she'd seen on his face since she'd met him.

"You're very good," he said to her.

She made a face. "I thought you'd be preoccupied enough to give me something."

"We'd better get going," Locke said to Hawkes.

"Why?" Hawkes asked. "They can't start without either one of us."

"I want to make sure everything is in place."

"Okay," Hawkes said. "From the looks of the people going by the café, the rest of the town is down there already."

Locke stood up and said, "Yeah, that's what worries me."

FIFTY-EIGHT

Locke decided that he and Hawkes would take Nina Ballinger with them to the sheriff's office. There she could talk to the new lawman, and even the judge. On the way they told her what had happened the night before, how Vestal had been killed.

"Oh, my God," she said, as they joined the stream of people heading toward the gallows. "Why didn't you tell me this last night?"

"It was late," Hawkes said.

"Then why not this morning? This is big news!"

"Big as the hanging?" Locke asked.

"Maybe."

"Well then, afterward you can write about both. Right now you can talk with the new sheriff and the man who appointed him."

"Poor Ed," she said, shaking her head.

"Ed?"

"Ed Hansen, Gordon's partner," she said. "He'll never survive out here without Vestal."

"You don't think Hansen was in on Vestal's deal with Colon?" Locke asked.

"I'm not at all surprised that Vestal was in cahoots with the bandits," she said, "but I'd be shocked if Ed Hansen knew about it."

"It didn't exactly strike me as an equal partnership," Locke said.

"It wasn't. Oh, maybe on paper, but Vestal made all the decisions and told Hansen what do. Without Vestal to guide him, he's finished."

"If Vestal was making money from the bandidos," Locke said, "chances are he was stealing from his partner, too. Hansen's going to be better off without him."

"I guess you'll have to try convincing him of that," Hawkes said.

"Or convincing the judge that Hansen was in the dark," Locke said.

People surged around them as they got closer to the gallows. Hawkes had his new pistol tucked into his belt, and was carrying his rifle. Locke was wearing his Peacemaker, and had the newly purchased gun tucked into his belt. He knew that the big hangman was cutting down on the length of his stride to accommodate Locke's limping pace, and appreciated it.

"Nina," Locke said.

"Yes?"

"Do you have a gun?"

"Actually," she said, digging into her purse, "I do." She produced a Sharps four-barrel .32 caliber "pepperbox" pistol with ivory grips. A lady's gun, to be sure, but the caliber was large enough to do some damage.

"Do you know how to use that?" Locke asked.

"Yes, I do," she said, putting it back. "It was a gift from an admirer. He also taught me how to shoot."

"Keep it handy," Locke advised. "You might need it."

"Maybe I can be of some assistance, then," she suggested.

"That's possible," Locke said.

"We could use all the help we can get," Hawkes said.

When they reached the area of the scaffolding a crowd had already gathered around it. Off to one side a drummer had set up his wagon and was selling his souvenirs. In another area one of the saloons had set up a makeshift bar and was serving beer at double the usual price.

"It looks like a damn circus is in town," Locke muttered.

"Come on," Hawkes said, "I'll make a path through the crowd."

With Nina between them they made their way through the crowd, Hawkes using his big body to clear a path to the sheriff's office. When they reached the door they found a large group of people standing there, waiting with a deputy.

"What's going on?" Locke asked.

"They say they have invitations," the deputy said.

Locke faced the group, which was made up of adults of all ages, and a few children. A few of them waved the invitations at him.

Locke turned to the deputy and said, "Make sure anyone with an invitation gets seated in the viewing stand— and no one else."

"What if some others try to—"

"Take another man," Locke said, cutting him off. "Get these people seated, and then get back here."

"Yes, sir."

They opened the door and allowed Nina to enter first. Inside they found Judge Tinsley, along with Sheriff James, Ben Ames, and a few other men milling about.

"One of you go out and help the other deputy."

One of the other deputies nodded and went out.

"What is she doing here?" Judge Tinsley demanded.

"Her job," Locke said.

"I don't want her—"

"She stays, Judge," Locke said, cutting the man off. "You two may be on opposite sides of some political fence, but I'm in charge here. She's going to cover this for her newspaper. The public has a right to know."

"You don't know what you're talking about," the judge said, "but fine. She can't do much damage now."

Hawkes was peering out the window and said, "Looks to me like the whole public is out there, waiting to see this."

Locke looked at the new sheriff, Gavin James.

"What about your men?" he asked.

"Six, and Mr. Ames, here."

"I thought you had eight?"

"Uh, two haven't shown up . . . yet."

"Did you swear in all six?"

"Didn't have enough badges to go around, but yeah, they're all sworn in."

"Good."

"Where's Doc Holliday?" James asked.

"He'll be here."

"He'll have to be sworn in—" the judge started.

"No," Locke said.

"What? Why not?"

"I'm not being sworn in, and Doc won't. He's here as my friend."

"And Hawkes?"

"He's the hangman," Locke said. "Doesn't have to be sworn in, either." He looked at James. "You really think your other two will show?"

James shrugged. "Maybe they were just caught up in the moment yesterday. Although I think I'd rather have Doc Holliday than those two."

"I agree," Locke said.

"Holliday's the lunger, right?" Judge Tinsley asked.

"He's a man, and my friend," Locke said.

"I meant no disrespect," Tinsley added hurriedly. "I just meant, if he's in poor health, he might not be able to make it through that mob."

"He'll make it," Hawkes said. "People tend to give Doc leeway."

At that moment the door opened. They all expected it to be Doc Holliday but instead Ed Hansen walked in carrying a rifle.

"What are you doing here?" the judge demanded.

"I feel partly responsible," Hansen said.

"For what?" Locke asked.

Hansen turned a hangdog look Locke's way.

"I didn't know that my partner was in with Colon," he said. "I feel like a fool. I want to help."

"You'll get killed—" Tinsley started.

"Can you fire that thing?" Locke asked, cutting the judge off once more.

"I can."

Locke looked at the sheriff.

"He wants to make amends and it's okay with me. The more guns we have, the better."

"It's okay with me, too," James said. "I can put a man at each end of town. At first sight of the bandidos they'll come a-running."

"Don't bother. We can't afford to split up our forces. Believe me, when they get here we'll know. Why don't you get your other men into position?"

"Right."

"Hansen, you go with them. You, too, Ben. When the two deputies get back from across the street take them with you."

Both men nodded and gripped their weapons. They filed out of the room behind the deputies. Locke recognized the two men who had helped Gavin James build the gallows.

"When do we go?" James asked Locke.

"You ready?" Locke asked Hawkes.

"My rope is still out there after testing it last night."

"With a sack of potatoes," Locke reminded him. "Will it hold?"

"Oh, it'll hold."

"Bring him out, then," Locke said to James. "We might as well get this over with."

"Right."

"We'll walk him out with you."

James nodded and went to get the prisoner.

"I'll walk with you," Judge Tinsley said.

"Judge, this could be—"

"—dangerous? I'm armed." He brushed back his coat to reveal a holstered Colt on his right hip. "I won't ask you men to do anything I wouldn't do myself."

Locke studied the man for a moment, and then said, "That's fair."

FIFTY-NINE

Hawkes went out the door first, followed by the judge, then Ignacio Colon pushed from behind by Sheriff Gavin James. Locke started out, then turned and faced Nina Ballinger.

"You stay here."

"What? I thought you said—"

"I said you could cover it for your paper," he said, cutting her short. "If you stand right here you'll be able to see everything. If you get out in that crowd and something happens you might get trampled, or worse."

She stared at him a moment, then said, "You expect a riot, don't you?"

"I expect trouble," he said, "and with this many people . . . well, that just makes it worse."

"A lot of people are likely to get hurt, then," she said. "Why didn't you keep them away?"

He stared at her. "How would you have suggested I do that? This town is chomping at the bit for this hanging."

"You could have had it somewhere else."

"If we tried to move Colon to another jurisdiction, by horseback or wagon, these people would have dragged him off and strung him up. They want this done right here in their own town."

"But they're going to get hurt."

"It's a possibility, Nina, but the risk is their choice."

"Can I quote you when it's all over?" she asked, bitterly.

"Yes."

Her eyes brightened. "Really?"

"Yes. Now stay here."

But she had already taken out a pad and paper and was writing furiously. He lifted his gun an inch or so out of his holster, just to be sure it wouldn't stick, then dropped it down again. He left her and went to catch up to the others.

Carlos Mendoza called for the bandidos to halt.

"What is it, Carlos?" Hernando Juarez asked.

"When we ride over that rise," Mendoza answered, "we will be visible from Fredericksburg."

"Sí," Juarez said.

"If they are smart they will have a lookout," Mendoza said. "He will warn them that we are coming."

"What do we do?"

"Who is our best marksman?" Mendoza asked.

"Ignacio was."

"I mean, of the men we have with us."

Juarez turned in his saddle to look behind him.

"Diego and Paco."

"Do we have Ignacio's rifle?"

"Sí."

Colon had left behind his Sharps Big .50, the buffalo rifle he had taken from a former buffalo hunter several years ago. He had become very proficient with the large rifle.

"Can Diego or Paco use it?" Mendoza asked.

Juarez thought a moment, then said, "Diego, I think."

"Then Diego and I will go up the rise on foot. If we can locate the lookout, he will take one shot to try to kill him."

"If he succeeds?"

"We will ride into town."

"And if he fails? And the lookout alerts El Viudador?"

Mendoza looked at Juarez. "We will ride in, anyway. Whether or not they know we are coming, we will ride right into town, crushing anyone who gets in our way."

"Then why take the shot at the lookout?"

"If we kill him it will make our task that much easier," Mendoza said, "but either way, Fredericksburg will be sorry we came."

"No lookout, Carlos," he reported.

"They are fools," Hernando Juarez said, as Diego once again mounted his horse.

"Perhaps not."

"Why?"

"Because when we ride in we will be announcing our own arrival," Mendoza said. "It will be no secret to anyone—least of all El Viudador."

SIXTY

Locke mounted the gallows awkwardly with the sheriff and the prisoner, dragging his bad leg up behind him. Arlo Hawkes was up there already, waiting. So was the hangman's noose.

At the top of the stairs Locke turned and faced Ignacio Colon.

"Still think this isn't going to happen?"

Colon stared back at him, trying to remain stoic, but Locke could see that just behind that gaze was panic waiting to get out. The brash outlaw was getting ready to crack. For some reason, Locke found himself hoping Colon could hold it together long enough to hang with dignity.

He turned his back as Arlo Hawkes fit the noose over Colon's head and regarded the milling crowd. The looks on their faces were, for the most part, hungry. They wanted this badly. He caught sight of some men and women huddled close to each other across the street, expressionless. He also looked over at the family members on the viewing stand, who had come to watch the outlaw who had murdered their loved ones pay for what he had done. There was no hunger in their eyes, unless it was for justice.

And that was when he heard the thundering hooves.

Locke wasn't the only one to hear the approaching horses. Many in the crowd heard them and turned to see what was happening. Before they knew it the bandidos had ridden down on them, trampling innocent bystanders beneath their horses' hooves . . . and then the shooting started!

"Here we go!" Locke shouted at Hawkes.

Locke pulled both guns while Hawkes groped for his rifle, which he had laid down to free his hands to do his job. Judge Tinsley also produced his pistol. All three men brandished their weapons and waited to locate targets.

Doc Holliday was hurrying along the boardwalk as quickly as he could, concerned that he would not only be late for the hanging, but that he would be letting down both of his friends, Locke and Hawkes. He was coughing into a white handkerchief when the bandidos rode by him. He put the cloth away, pulled his gun, and quickened his pace.

The bandidos had ridden in at full speed but as they reached the crowd their progress was slowed tremendously. A couple of the horses stumbled and a few men were thrown from their saddles and into the crowd. Other bandits fired into the crowd to protect their fallen comrades.

* * *

Carlos Mendoza could plainly see the scaffolding up ahead, and recognized Ignacio Colon immediately. There were four other men standing there with him whom he didn't recognize, but they all had guns and it was not difficult to figure out their identities. The hangman, the sheriff, the judge, and El Viudador.

"Never mind the crowd!" he shouted to his men in Spanish. "Do not fire at them! Fire at the gallows."

"Carlos!" Juarez said, riding up alongside him. "We might hit Ignacio!"

Mendoza turned to look at Juarez, grabbed the front of his shirt, and shouted, "Then make sure you do not."

From their vantage point on the gallows, there initially would have been no danger of firing at the bandidos and hitting people in the crowd. But now they were wading through the mob on their horses, trying to get closer to the scaffolding, and firing at them meant the possibility of killing bystanders.

"Hold your fire!" Locke shouted, mostly for the benefit of the judge and the sheriff. He was confident that he and Hawkes would hit what they aimed at. The other two might miss, and their bullets would bypass the bandits and strike the citizens behind them. "Don't fire unless you have a definite target—and don't miss!"

"When they get closer we can spring our trap!" Sheriff James called back.

Hawkes turned and looked at the new lawman, then at Locke.

"Do you see what I see?" he asked.

"Yeah," Locke said, "and it's going to be a problem."

Once they sprang their trap they'd be outgunned, but at least the element of surprise would be on their side.

SIXTY-ONE

Suddenly the air was filled with flying lead. Locke's first shot took a bandido right from his saddle. From across the street he saw Doc Holliday firing over the heads of the crowd. Next to him he heard Hawkes's rifle being fired, and from behind him the sheriff and the judge let loose their rounds.

The bandits were still pushing through the crowd which, instead of dispersing, for some reason was surging toward the gallows. This was what both Hawkes and Locke had noticed.

This was not a good sign.

Beneath the gallows, hidden by the walls Gavin James had added at the request of Locke, Deputy Bill Rabb heard the shooting. He knew it was their cue to move.

"Let's go," he said. He and the men with him were to push at the walls, which were constructed to fall outward, away from the gallows. These men would then surprise the bandidos with their presence, the element of surprise intended to help them gain an advantage that would make up for their lack of numbers.

Rabb and several of the men pushed against the wooden wall, but it wouldn't budge. The crowd outside was leaning against it, holding it in place.

"What the hell—" one of the new deputies swore.

"Jesus," Rabb said. "We're trapped in here."

"Let's try over there," one of the men shouted, and they moved to another side but found the same problem. The crowd outnumbered them, keeping them pinned inside.

Trapped beneath the gallows they were safe, but outside the sheriff and the others would be hopelessly outnumbered.

"We gotta get out of here!" Rabb shouted.

"They're trapped inside!" Hawkes shouted to Locke.

Locke was firing with both hands and Doc was still firing from across the street, but they were the only two who seemed to be shooting with any accuracy. Locke had already seen members of the crowd go down from random fire, but it couldn't be helped. It was a cruel thought, but if they'd stayed home instead of coming out to watch a man hang they would have been safe.

"We've got to clear the crowd away so the men can get out," Locke called back. "Without them we're dead."

They could feel the scaffolding vibrating beneath them as the men trapped beneath pounded on the sides. They were in no danger down there, but were of no help, either.

On the other hand, if the bandidos succeeded in freeing Ignacio Colon, killing Locke, Hawkes, and the others in the process, then the men would be sitting ducks. The bandits could shoot them at will or, worse, set fire to the scaffolding.

But rather than think that way—and rather than stand there wasting time thinking—they had to get them out.

"Gavin!" Locke shouted.

The sheriff looked over at him.

"Get down there and try to help them out. Get the people away from there!"

"Right."

Gavin James holstered his gun and ran down the steps of the gallows. Once on the ground he tried to get between the people and the scaffolding to force people back, but it was no good. There were just too many of them, and their weight was too great. The only thing he couldn't figure was why they were moving closer to the gallows rather than trying to run away.

Then, suddenly, he had an idea.

Locke felt a bullet tug at his sleeve, the second such nibble lead had taken from him. He knew he was bleeding, though not badly. He looked over at Hawkes and saw that the big man, too, was bleeding from a couple of minor hits.

"If some of these damned people would draw guns and start shooting it sure would help!" Hawkes shouted.

Locke turned to look behind him. the judge was down on one knee, having taken a more serious injury. He also saw Colon, who was watching the proceeding with the rope around his neck, standing on the trapdoor. His eyes were wide, but Locke could not tell if it was with triumph, or panic.

"Judge," Locke said, backing up and crouching by the man.

"I'm all right," the older man said, but Locke could see the blood flowing from between the man's fingers as he clutched at his upper thigh. Hurriedly, he removed the man's belt.

"What the hell—" Tinsley said, but Locke ignored him. He wrapped the belt around the judge's thigh above the wound as he'd once seen a doctor do. "Hold this tight with one hand, and shoot with the other. We'll take care of it later."

"If there is a later," the judge said through gritted teeth.

Locke didn't reply. If James didn't find a way to free the rest of the men the judge might be right.

SIXTY-TWO

Gavin James ran back around the gallows and under the stairs. The other three side panels had been nailed in only a few places, so that the men underneath would be able to push them out easily. This side, however, he had nailed securely because he didn't think they'd be using it. Now, with the crowds pushing against the other three, this seemed the easiest way out. The crowd had not discovered the area beneath the steps, for some reason.

Sheriff James began banging on this side to attract the attention of the men inside.

Bill Rabb was looking around in a panic. He and Ben Ames, the bartender, both heard the pounding on the wall of the gallows beneath the stairs, despite the noise of the crowd and the shots. They ran to it and put their ears to the wood.

"Push this side!" they both heard Gavin James shouting. "This . . . side!"

The two men exchanged a glance, and then started yelling at the same time for the other men to join them. Six shoulders began slamming into the wood, and the shrieking of nails could be heard as the jarring impact loosened them.

Locke could still feel the pounding beneath them, but it seemed to have shifted. He knelt to reload and thought that the impact was coming from the area beneath the stairs.

Several bandidos lay dead among the crowd, either shot or trampled when they fell from their horses, but Doc, Hawkes, and Locke were still outnumbered. the judge had keeled over and was now holding his leg. The bandits were still pushing through the crowd, and getting dangerously close to the gallows. Without the help of the half dozen men beneath them they couldn't hold out much longer.

Doc Holliday felt helpless. He was firing at the bandidos, but he was being buffeted from all sides now that some of the crowd had joined him on the boardwalk. His shots were going wild and he was being no help to the men atop the scaffolding. He needed to gain firmer footing for himself.

Where the hell was this trap Locke had planned?

Carlos Mendoza knew they were moments away from reaching the men on the gallows. One had fallen already, another had run down the stairs, possibly fleeing for his life. That left two there with Colon, the hangman, and John Locke. He was also aware of another man firing at them from across the street, whose aim was being hampered by the crowd. Some of his men were firing back, hitting people around him, but not the man himself. Mendoza didn't think it mattered, though. The man looked like a ghost, like a walking dead man. He decided that this man was of no consequence and turned his attention back to the scaffolding.

The crowd puzzled him. Instead of running, most of them had moved closer to the gallows, as if it would offer them some shelter. Fools. If he chose to he could massacre many of the townspeople. Already some lay dead or injured in the street, and that was enough for him. All that remained was for him to achieve his final goal.

He shouted to his men, not really forming any words but just urging them to continue their surge toward the gallows.

Sheriff James could feel the barrier coming looser and looser, the nails finding less and less purchase as the men on the other side continued to throw their combined weight at it.

Any moment now, he thought, any moment.

Locke was getting to the point where he was tempted to fire at the people in the crowd who were seemingly adhering to the sides of the gallows. What could they possibly be thinking? Why weren't they running for their homes, or for cover?

And then he realized what it was. It made no sense to him, but he knew he must be right. They had come here to see a hanging. They weren't leaving without one.

SIXTY-THREE

The nails finally gave and the wall began to come down— only to be stopped by the stairs. For a moment Gavin James panicked but there was room on either side and the men began to scamper out, drawing their guns, glad to finally be part of the action.

"Stay on the ground," he shouted, "don't climb the gallows. Use the people for cover."

Ben Ames stared at him.

"They'll be killed."

"Some of them will be, anyway," James said, "but when they see you, shooting at the bandidos and being shot at, it may cause them to finally go for cover and disperse."

"We could use some help here!" Locke called down the stairs.

"Go!" James said, and ran back up. "They're out!" he called to Locke.

At that moment the men appeared among the crowd and began firing at the bandidos, the element of surprise still on their side.

*　*　*

A hail of bullets flew at Colon's men, knocking a man from his saddle on either side of Carlos Mendoza and Hernando Juarez.

"They have more men!" Juarez shouted. "Where did they come from?"

Mendoza looked around. The street was littered with bodies, some belonging to his own men. From what he could see his forces had been cut in half, and suddenly Locke's forces had tripled in size. The bandidos still outnumbered the lawmen, but not by very much.

"We have to get to Ignacio!" Juarez shouted.

Suddenly, a bullet struck Juarez in the throat. He sat astride his horse, shocked. Turning his head to look at Mendoza he opened his mouth to speak, but a great gout of blood came forth instead. Juarez slid from his horse and was dead before he hit the ground. Mendoza saw that it was the walking dead man who had killed Juarez.

"The crowd!" he shouted, suddenly. "Fire into the crowd."

If he could get Locke and the others concerned with the crowd it might hinder their efforts.

"Carlos—" one of his men called.

"Kill as many of them as you can!"

Locke saw what Mendoza was doing. He'd watched Doc take a bead and fire, taking a man from his saddle with a well-placed shot to the throat. The man had been side by side with another man Locke took to be the temporary leader, and might have been his segundo. This caused the man to call out to his men, and suddenly the guns were trained on the crowd.

"They're gonna start killing people, John!" Hawkes shouted.

"I know," Locke said.

"What do we do?"

Locke stared at Hawkes, then looked over at Colon, who was still standing on the trapdoor with the noose around his neck, his hands tied behind him. There was some blood on him, indicating he had taken a hit or two, but he was still alive. The bandidos had come to save him, the crowd had come to watch him hang. It seemed that no one was going to leave while he was alive.

Suddenly, without warning, Locke turned and kicked out. His boot hit the lever that controlled the trapdoor. It opened and Ignacio Colon fell through. He had gone only several feet when suddenly the noose pulled tight. Even using a sack of potatoes to test the gallows Hawkes had gotten it right. Locke heard the sound of Colon's neck crack, and then the man was hanging there, dead.

As if they knew what was happening, the crowd moved away from the gallows, backing up to get a better look. In so doing they released the barriers on all three sides of the gallows, which fell, opening the underside of the gallows to everyone's view. There, for all to see, was Ignacio Colon, still swinging. He was not kicking, and his neck was at an odd angle.

The shooting stopped. The quiet was total for a moment. Then there was moaning from the injured, and the creaking of the gallows as the man swung back and forth. Someone shouted, "He's dead!" triumphantly, and the crowd roared.

"What do we do now, Carlos?" one of Mendoza's men asked.

What, indeed? There was no longer an Ignacio Colon to rescue. The man was hanging by the neck, dead. Carlos Mendoza was now the permanent leader of the bandidos—what was left of them.

The realization that Colon was dead did not distress him. Indeed, he thought he had probably come to town to make sure Colon hanged, not to save him. After all, he had taken a great liking to being the leader.

And now the deed was done. Colon was dead, he was in charge, and he had to protect what men he had left.

"Let's get out of here!" he shouted.

Locke, Hawkes, and James stared as the bandidos turned and rode off. A few of the deputies threw shots at them as they galloped away.

"Where are they going?" James asked. "They still have the upper hand."

"There's nothing left to fight for," Locke said, "that's why they're leaving. They came to rescue Colon, and he's dead."

"Jesus," James said, turning and looking at the hanging man, "you mean that was all we had to do? Spring the door and they'd leave?"

"That's it," Locke said. Secretly, he cursed himself for

not realizing this sooner. There were bodies in the street, most of them ordinary citizens. Perhaps this could have been avoided if, upon the arrival of the bandidos in town, he had simply sprung the door and executed Ignacio Colon on the spot.

Doc Holliday came sauntering across the street, reloading as the crowd now parted for him. Most of them were actually going home, others stood and gaped at the swaying man. Still others saw to their neighbors and friends, or family, on the street. A few pulled the bandidos who were still alive to their feet, and began kicking the ones who were dead.

Locke turned to Gavin James and said, "Sheriff, we need the doctor."

SIXTY-FOUR

Locke squinted at the morning sun as he came out of his hotel the next day. The streets were clean, no bodies, either lying down or walking around. Apparently, people were staying in their homes in the aftermath of yesterday's bloodbath.

"They should have stayed home yesterday," Arlo Hawkes said, coming out of the hotel and standing next to him, "not today."

Locke looked over at Hawkes, who had a morning edition of the *Front Page* in his hands.

"How many does she say were killed?"

"Ten dead, twice that many injured from being either shot or trampled."

"And bandidos?"

"Ten dead. In a separate story she talks about Ignacio Colon being executed, as scheduled."

"Yeah," Locke said, "scheduled. What about the judge?"

"She reports he was shot but that he'll survive. He's at home."

"Then that's where we have to go," Locke said.

"For what?"

"To get paid."

Hawkes put a big hand on his friend's shoulder.

"You think you're gonna get the rest of your money?" he asked.

"Oh," Locke said, "I'm going to get paid, and so are you. Come on."

As they walked through town to the judge's house Hawkes asked, "How did you sleep?"

"Like a baby." It was a lie, and they both knew it.

"You put some demons to rest yesterday, didn't you?" the hangman asked.

"I guess I did."

Locke had overseen the cleanup of the streets, bodies removed, injured people taken over to the doctor. There had been some property damage, as well, mostly windows shattered by bullets, or bodies falling through them. It was obvious the adults had managed to protect the children. The only dead he saw were adults. Leaning over several men were their wives, who looked up at him as he passed, their eyes blaming him. After all, they were now widows, weren't they? But Locke wasn't going to take the blame— not all of it, anyway. After all, they could have stayed safe in their homes, and he personally had not shot any of them.

It had taken most of the day to get everything cleaned up, including having Ignacio Colon's body taken to the undertaker. After it was all done he had gone to his hotel room and sat down on his bed. He expected the shakes to follow, but they never came. Neither did the desire for a beer or a whiskey. He didn't know how permanent that was, but it hadn't returned yet and he was grateful for the respite.

"Guess you know what kind of man you are," Hawkes said, "again. It's been . . . what, five years since Tombstone? It's nice to have you back."

"It's nice to be back," John Locke said.

The judge's wife answered Locke's knock on the front door. The Tinsley home was clearly the largest house in town, a well-kept wooden structure, two stories high, which had been painted recently.

"Yes?"

"John Locke to see Judge Tinsley."

"The judge is resting," she said. "He can't be—"

"Ma'am, I'm sure you know who I am."

"I do," she said, with clear distaste. She was a gray-haired woman in her fifties who had clearly once been a very handsome woman, but time had passed her by so that she now looked faded and unhappy.

"Well then, you know that my job is finished here in Fredericksburg. I would like to leave town, and to do that I need to be paid the rest of my money."

"The judge can't pay you—"

"Ma'am, he's the man in charge. My friend and I need to see him so somebody can pay us, and we can be on our way. You would like us to leave town, wouldn't you?"

She stared at him a moment, then said, "Wait here."

"What's she got against us?" Hawkes asked.

"We're not on her husband's side of the bench."

She reappeared moments later and said, "Please come in."

She allowed them to enter, then led them to a room filled with books. Her husband was sitting in an over-stuffed chair in a dressing gown, his injured leg up on a padded footstool.

"Mr. Locke and Mr. Hawkes," Tinsley said. "I suppose you've come for the remainder of your money."

"Mr. Hawkes hasn't been paid anything," Locke said, "and yes, I need to get the rest of my money."

"Well, gentlemen," Judge Tinsley said, "I'm afraid we have a problem there."

"There shouldn't be any problems, Judge," Locke said, tightly. "All fees were agreed to beforehand."

"Yes, yes," the judge said, "but who could have pre-dicted what would happen yesterday? The loss of life, the injuries, the property damage—"

"None of that is my concern," Locke said.

"Or mine," Hawkes said.

"But gentlemen, certainly you admit you caused it."

"I don't admit that at all, Judge," Locke said. "If anyone is to blame it's you."

"Me?"

"If Fredericksburg had a proper sheriff from the begin-ning you wouldn't have needed to hire me. If you'd exe-cuted Colon when you first caught him, none of this would have happened."

"Now see here—"

"No, Judge," Locke said, harshly, "you see here!" His

tone caused the judge's wife to start and she moved closer to her husband's chair to put a supportive hand on his shoulder. He ignored her and glared at Locke.

"You're not going to renege on our deal, Judge. And you're not going to stiff your hangman."

"You brought Mr. Hawkes here—"

Locke started toward the judge but was caught from behind by Arlo Hawkes's large hands.

"Easy," the hangman said. "I'm sure the judge wants to be sensible."

"You can't threaten me—"

"The only thing I'll threaten you with is a newspaper story about how you refused to pay what you owe," Locke said. "How you botched the execution of Ignacio Colon. I'm sure Nina Ballinger would be only too happy to print all the details."

"That bitch! You don't know anything about her, Locke. Did you know that Vestal was her lover?"

He didn't know that, but she did seem too good to be true to him most of the time. As for Vestal, he seemed to have formed alliances wherever he thought they could do him some good.

"Vestal was in with her, and with Colon—"

"And you're going to tell me you had no alliance with him?"

"Of course not—"

"I'll bet Ed Hansen would tell me different."

"Hansen," the judge said. "He didn't know—I mean, what would he know—"

"And I'll bet that although Vestal had an alliance with

Miss Ballinger, and with you, that you and she had no such arrangement. She'd be only too happy to interview you about everything that was going on behind the scenes of this little drama."

"Now, now," Tinsley said, leaning back in his chair and adopting a more relaxed attitude, "there's no need for threats, Mr. Locke. Believe me, the town intends to pay you, but much of that money was to come from Gordon Vestal and since he's dead—"

"—his partner inherits everything, right? Vestal had no wife? No family?"

"That's, er, correct—"

"Then there shouldn't be a problem, should there?"

The judge hesitated, but then his wife said, "Pay them, dear, pay them so they'll go away and we can get back to normal."

"Normal?" Locke asked. "You had a member of your Town Council working with Ignacio Colon and his bandidos to set up robberies, and you call that normal? How about if that makes it into the papers—"

"My dear," Judge Tinsley said, "fetch my checkbook from the desk, will you, please?" As she hurried to do so Tinsley said, "You have only to take these checks to the bank to collect your money, gentlemen. After that I assume you'll be leaving town?"

"Just as fast as we can, Judge," Locke assured him, "just as fast as we can."

When they came out of the bank they found Sheriff James waiting for them.

"I wanted to thank you gents for what you did," he said, putting out his hand.

"Just did what we were paid to do," Locke said as the new lawman shook his hand, and then Hawkes's.

"You weren't paid to get me appointed sheriff," James said to Locke. "I got you to thank for that."

Locke and Hawkes became aware of some banging coming from down the street.

"Takin' down the gallows," James explained. "I hope we won't need it again."

"If you ever do," Locke said, "don't call me."

Sheriff James touched his fingers to his hat brim and walked off down the street.

"Where's Doc?" Locke asked.

"Probably still in his room," Hawkes said. "He don't get up so easy anymore."

"He doesn't look like he has very long," Locke commented.

"Then again," Hawkes said, "he's looked like that for quite a while."

"I suppose," Locke said. "Well, I can't leave without saying good-bye to him and making sure he's all right. Not after he came to help without being asked."

"What about Nina?" Hawkes asked. "You gonna say good-bye to her?"

"No," Locke said. "You?"

"All that stuff you said about her true?"

"I'm sure it is," Locke said. "This town has done everything it can to prove me right, Arlo. Towns are fine for some people, but then other people start running them and they go to hell. Alliances, backstabbing, Town Councils . . ." he said, shaking his head and trailing off. "I've had it with them."

"You'd think Tombstone would have taught you a lesson," Hawkes said.

Locke looked at the big man, who for a moment thought maybe he'd gone too far, but then his friend said, "Yeah, you'd think."

EPILOGUE ONE

Glenwood Springs, Colorado
November 7, 1887

It was day fifty-six for Doc Holliday. That was how long he had been in bed at the Glenwood Springs Sanatorium. John Locke knew Doc Holliday had come west maintaining that he would never die in bed. During the early days of their friendship in Tombstone Doc had often said that he would die from a bullet, a knife, or at the end of a rope. He even said he might drink himself to death. But he never expected to die in bed, coughing up blood and guts.

Locke had heard just recently that Doc was in Glenwood Springs. If he had known he would have come sooner. He could count his good friends on the fingers of one hand, and Doc was usually the first finger.

Locke presented himself at the front desk and announced he was there to see Doc Holliday.

"Who?" the middle-aged nurse asked.

"John Henry Holliday?"

"Oh, yes, John Henry."

"Can I see him?"

"Well . . . there's a visitor in with him right now."

"Can't I go in anyway?"

"I don't see why not," she said, after a moment. "But you should know he might be delirious. He might not recognize you."

"I'll take that chance," Locke said. "I'd just like a moment."

"Are you a relative?"

"No, just a friend."

"You're only the second person to come and visit him." She rose. "Follow me, please."

He followed the nurse down a long hallway until she stopped in front of a door and said, "In here."

"Thank you."

Locke entered. Doc had a private room, and there was a man standing by his bed, looking down at him. He was tall, dressed in a dark suit, a majestic mustache hanging from a mournful face. He had his hands clasped in front of him, his black hat hanging from the fingers of one.

Behind the tall man was a window, and if Doc had been awake he could have looked out at green rolling hills.

"Wyatt," Locke said.

Wyatt Earp looked up, surprised for a moment, then saw Locke and nodded. "Hello, Locke."

Locke walked to the bed, stood on the other side. He studied Doc, whose eyes were closed. His face was almost as pale as the white sheets he was lying on. Never a large man, his body hardly seemed a visible hump beneath the sheets.

"How is he?" Locke asked.

"He's been out of it since I got here this morning. Yesterday we talked for a while."

"The nurse told me he's delirious sometimes."

"Couple of days ago he didn't know who I was," Wyatt said, nodding.

"How many days have you been here?"

"Just three," the tall man said. "Came as soon as I heard, though."

"So did I."

"Doc's not one to announce his business."

Locke nodded his agreement. He had not seen Doc since Fredericksburg, Texas, when he and Arlo Hawkes had helped get Ignacio Colon hanged. He'd heard a story or two about Doc's escapades, a couple of near misses where someone tried to ambush him, but their paths had not crossed since then.

"When did you see him last?"

"A few months ago," Wyatt said. "He looked like he could hardly stand then. Told me he might be coming up here to try the sulfur springs. Guess they're not helping much."

"He must be mad as hell," Locke said. "He expected to be long dead by now."

"I know," Wyatt said, "but believe it or not he's not mad. He thinks it's ironic."

The two men stood there, staring down at their mutual friend, as time ticked by, and then finally looked at each other again.

"He ain't comin' out of this today," Wyatt said. "How about lettin' me buy you a steak?"

"Can we come back tonight?"

Wyatt shook his head. "Visitors' hours will be over. We can come back in the mornin', though."

Locke looked down at Doc one more time, then said, "A steak sounds good. I've got to get a hotel room, too."

"We can get both at the same place," Wyatt said. "Come on, I'll show you."

They passed the nurse on the way out and she nodded her approval to them. The poor man, she thought. John Henry had not had a visitor in over fifty days, and now two within three. She hoped that these two men were very good friends of his. John Henry Holliday, she knew, did not have many more days left to him.

EPILOGUE TWO

Wyatt showed Locke to the hotel in town and waited while he checked in and stowed his gear in his room. After that they went into the hotel dining room.

"Food's actually not bad," Wyatt said.

"It'll be fine," Locke said. Food was secondary, this time around. It was more important to be staying somewhere close to Doc so he could see him as much as possible before he . . .

The waiter came over and they each ordered dinner.

"I want you to know," Wyatt said, "I thought you got mistreated in Tombstone."

"Thanks."

"No, I mean it," Wyatt said. "You kept the lid on that town as marshal. Once you left things got out of hand."

"Virgil was a good lawman," Locke said.

"Ah," Wyatt said, "my brothers and I, we got too personally involved. You were right."

"About what?"

"I heard that when you left you said Tombstone would erupt."

"I gave it six months."

"Happened in a year," Wyatt said. "Same difference."

"You and your brothers were lucky you had Doc."

"You can say that again," Wyatt said. "After you left, Doc and me, we got pretty friendly."

"I'm glad," Locke said. "Doc was never one to make friends easily."

"I know," Wyatt said. "Morg and Virgil didn't take to him, and neither did my friend Bat Masterson. Doc and I, though, we just sort of . . . saw eye to eye. I don't know that he ever had any other friends besides you and me."

"Arlo Hawkes."

"The hangman?"

Locke nodded. "I think that's it, though. Just the three of us."

"Hawkes must not know he's here."

"If he did he'd be here."

"Do you know where he is?" Wyatt asked. "We could send him a telegram."

The waiter came then with their meals and set them down in front of them.

"Want a beer?" Wyatt asked.

Locke shook his head. "Coffee."

The waiter went off to get their drinks.

"I might have a couple of ideas about Hawkes's whereabouts," Locke said. "I can send a couple of telegrams in the morning."

He cut into his steak, gathered up a bunch of onions, and shoved it all into his mouth.

"How is it?" Wyatt asked.

"It's good," Locke said. "It's good."

*   *   *

During dinner they talked about Doc, each telling his own stories.

"He was the most skillful gambler and the nerviest, fastest, deadliest man with a six-gun I ever saw," Wyatt said, at one point.

Locke had to agree. Hickok and Ben Thompson notwithstanding, Locke thought that Doc was the fastest man with a gun he had ever known. And oddly enough, for a man whose hands often shook too much to fire a gun, in a firefight he was the steadiest shot Locke had ever seen.

They both agreed they wouldn't want anyone else backing them up when the time came.

After dinner Wyatt said, "I'm going over to the saloon. Care to join me?"

"I'm kind of tired after riding all day," Locke said. "I think I'm just going to go to my room."

"How about meeting me for breakfast and then we'll go over and see Doc together?"

"Suits me," Locke said. "I hope he's alert enough to know who I am, and that I'm there."

"He will be, Locke," Wyatt said. "Let's hope he will."

After breakfast in the hotel dining room the next morning they saddled their horses and rode over to the sanatorium. The same nurse was sitting at the desk and smiled at them.

"You're very early," she said. "He's not awake yet."

They nodded to her and walked down the hall. It was

important to Locke that Doc knew he was there. He hoped today would be one of his friend's alert days.

He entered the room behind Wyatt. It was odd, but during his time in Tombstone Locke had not had much use for the Earps. Now, however, after just a few hours in the man's company, he felt that a bond may have formed. Maybe there was something about waiting together for a mutual friend to die.

They approached the bed and took up the same positions they had occupied the night before. At that moment Doc Holliday opened his eyes and looked at them. Amazingly, his usually bloodshot eyes were clear.

"Well, lookee here," he said. "All my friends are in one place."

"Hawkes would be here, but he doesn't know about your condition, Doc," Locke said.

"In fact we didn't know until recently," Wyatt said.

"What's it matter?" Doc asked. "I didn't need you gents to see me like this."

"We're your friends, Doc," Wyatt said.

"We're supposed to be here," Locke said.

"Well," Doc said, "one of you friends get me a drink, will you? There's a bottle in that top drawer."

Wyatt turned and opened the top drawer of the end table next to the bed. He took out a bottle of whiskey and a glass. He poured a shot and while Locke lifted Doc's head Wyatt helped him drink it. Neither man thought anything of the gentleness with which they aided their friend. Locke set Doc's head back down on the pillow and then John Henry Holliday laughed almost to himself, said, "This is funny," and died.